Flip

A novel by
Steve Stinson

FLIP by Steve Stinson

ISBN 978-1-957586-28-1

A Conservatarian Press Publication

Cover art by: Steve Stinson

Copyright 2023 Steve Stinson

Printed in the United States of America
Worldwide Electronic & Digital Rights
Worldwide English Language Print Rights

Conservatarian
Press

Dedicated to: Thou

Contents

I

CROSSROADS

I knew if I worked on the painting much longer, I would ruin it, so I kept at it.

It was August 1964 in a large old house in a small Nebraska town. It was what people call the middle of the night. The upstairs rooms were empty, except for the dust. Downstairs was furnished, more or less. There was a couch, but you wouldn't know it for the junk. It was an art studio, in its way. I also lived there, if you want to call it that.

Nothing was where it should be, or maybe everything wasn't supposed to be there. The floor was a swarming accident, a landscape of forsaken tokens, remnants of occasions and schemes. Possessions mingled with rubbish, or maybe they were the same. Road signs were nailed to the floor. They covered the holes. Clothing and books and ashtrays – none empty – and beer cans – none full – and car parts and tools and magazines and advertising signs and crumbs from needless feedings.

It wasn't personal. There was a church bulletin. I didn't go to church. There was a shoe. I didn't have its mate. There was a horseshoe. I didn't have a horse. Scrabble pieces and playing cards and Monopoly money scattered like confetti over the pile. I didn't play any of those games. There were puzzle pieces. I hate puzzles. There was a broken watch. I didn't wear jewelry. There was a padlock. I owned nothing of value. There were cigarette packages. Lots of them.

Smoking, I did.

There was a court summons. There were traffic tickets, lots of them. There were half-done, all-done, and maybe-done sketches and drawings and canvasses. The name "Matthew Andrews" was stamped on the summons and the tickets and signed on a few of the canvasses.

That's me.

An easel, hot lit by a swing arm lamp, spiked up from a clearing in the waste. There, I bent toward an oversized portrait of a young woman. It was a lovely, intuitive portrait that was also modernist. The style and handling were mature. The colors were like four-part harmony. It was bigger than it needed to be. The thing breathed confidence. I was eighteen years old.

Waist up, I had that studied, faux Elvis look, including the greased-up Chicago Boxcar hairstyle beloved by Fifties-era low-beam hoodlums. You had to work on that hair. You had to want it. Push it high on both sides and then pull it forward and down at the forehead. If it weren't for the strands that dangled in front – just so – you'd think it was made of asphalt. Waist down, I looked like a working cowboy, which I wasn't.

I was nose-in with my work. Truly. I should have stopped an hour before. My eyes were tired and my neck hurt and my arm ached and my fingers were stiff. I knew I was done because I had just nicked a little pile of paint off the canvas with a pocket knife. When you get careless about the load on your brush, it's time to put the brush down.

The last thing this painting needed was one more thing. My brush – I prefer the short flat rounded ones – and my turp-slick fingers were poised to add it.

My door slammed open. Abby scrambled in and sent the floorscape airborne. For a moment, I heard the music I always heard when she entered a room. She was slim and small and dark. She had aquiline features that danced between handsome and pretty. She was smart and quick and she was always straight with you, which was good because she did most of the thinking for us. She was the only person on earth who could stand me.

I looked into her eyes, and the music stopped. I saw white-hot fear. And then she saw the portrait, and the fear melted away. She stopped dead in front of it. It was her. Well, it was *of* her.

"You're doing Modigliani," she said. There was that pitch-perfect ding of delight in her voice. It was just what I wanted. She didn't have that F-sharp upper-Midwest-almost-Canada sound. She had a touch of Texas in her voice. Like sunflowers.

"You noticed," I said.

And like that, her fear returned. You could almost hear her pulse. She started corralling clothes and possessions from the floor. Flinging this. Gripping that. Riddling the forlorn scraps of my life.

"You've got to go. Get away. Now. This minute."

No pitch-perfect ding this time. It was followed by overwrought muttering, something like, "God, you're a mess."

I stepped away from the easel and watched as she dug paper bags from the clutter and stuffed them with clothes. Manic. She found a canvas bag. I could feel the crazy.

"What are you doing? What are you talking about?"

She didn't slow down. She moved to the clearing and hustled

3

art supplies into the canvas bag.

"They know, and they're on the way. Here. Now."

Quick brain reconnoiter. I had not done anything wrong for which I had not already been caught. At least not lately. I stopped her and spun her around before the easel and held her by the shoulders, which was difficult. I still had a palette in one hand and a brush in the other.

"Who are they? What do they know? Why are they coming?"

"The baby. They know about the baby. Dad and both my brothers."

You know, you can only pretend a true thing isn't true – especially if you can't see it or touch it – until that true thing gets very true. I let her go. I just stood there. She opened another bag. Manic again. Is it possible to feel fear and resolve and delusion at the same time? Yes.

"We'll get married."

I meant it, which surprised us both.

"Oh, for God's sake, Matt."

"I'll be nineteen next year. You'll be twenty-two."

She gave me her stop-the-madness look.

"Dad has a shotgun. It's not for a wedding."

Eye contact. She wasn't kidding. She'd been quick. I didn't own much worth keeping, and she'd rounded it up. She shoved the last bag at me. I held it with my elbows, my brush and palette askew.

My final dab of paint ended up on my cheek. Red. It smeared. She tried to push me away from the easel. It was the first time her touch repelled me. Ever.

I dropped the bag. "I'm not going anywhere. Nobody's gonna push me around."

"Oh, for God's sake, Matt."

Fear, resolve, and delusion again.

"I'll take 'em. All of 'em."

This wasn't altogether bluster. I could manage her two brothers. They would be itching for a fight. One was a lunatic. A little justifiable homicide was just what he'd want. I might even enjoy taking him out. The other would quit when the lunatic was finished. Her father, though, he was different. Even I knew he was right and I was wrong. That means something in a fight.

And then there was the shotgun.

She stopped and turned and gave me that look, the one that says too much about me. I really didn't like it when she acted like my mother, which, unfortunately, she was often required to do.

"Alone? And then what? Who's gonna take your side? You've pissed off everybody in this town except me."

This was true.

She hesitated in front of the portrait. She took it in and she softened and she gave me that other look. The one I liked.

"You captured me," she said. "Again."

I didn't miss the double entendre. And like that, and for the first time, I began to grasp how hard this was on her.

"You know," she said. "Sometimes I don't see how it's possible that you…"

Her arm swept the crime scene of my room.

"…and you…"

She stopped at the portrait.

"…are the same person."

And her trance passed.

"Go."

I put down the palette and brush and slipped a cigarette between my lips. Gave her my tough-guy look.

5

"No."

Abby dropped her bags and swiped the cigarette from my mouth and tossed it. She buried her head and shoulders in my chest and shoved harder, near hysteria. I didn't budge. She fell into me.

"Please don't do this. I'm begging you. For me. I don't know what they'll do. They're, just, just crazy."

I swaggered. Tough guy again. She backed away.

"Oh, for God's sake, Matt."

I grabbed her and held her until she settled down. I kissed her. We had a lot of practice at that. Abby began to wilt and then broke off the embrace.

"There's no time."

Then it came out of me. The words not to be spoken.

"The baby."

She gave me a look. This one was new to me.

"Matt, there isn't going to be a baby."

"What do you mean? How can there not be a baby?"

"Oh, for God's sake, Matt. There…isn't…going…to be…a baby."

She locked eyes with mine. I knew what she meant but I didn't know what she meant. This must have been written all over my face.

"It will be taken care of," she said. Her eyes never moved until she understood that I now had something new to pretend wasn't true. But she couldn't pretend. There was a catch in her voice when she said it. A tiny tremble, but enough that I could feel it. I could feel it enter me, but I didn't know where to put it.

"What about your father?" I said. "He won't let that happen."

"He won't know about it until too late," she said, and leveled her eyes at me again. I felt the catch in her voice again. I still didn't know where to put it.

Abby being tough. Abby being hard. Abby with a catch in her voice. Me being numb. We just looked at each other until her resolve returned, and she shoved me again. This time, I went along.

✳✳✳

Mine was the only rental house on an otherwise nice residential street. My truck, old and cranky and weary – no, I never named it – was at the curb. Abby piled the bags in the bed. It didn't take long. She moved fast. I just moved. The last thing to go in was the easel and the canvas bag with the art supplies. I took the bag and easel back out and dropped them at the curb.

"Keep them," I said.

Oil paint is expensive. So are brushes and easels and canvasses. She was the better painter. It just made sense to leave the bag. She wanted to refuse, I could tell. She made that little move she always made just before she was about to tell me how wrong I was, but she stopped. No time for corrections tonight. The bag and easel stayed at the curb. And then it was time.

We stood in the street by the truck. All I had to do was reach out and open the door, and all this would disappear behind me. I didn't give a damn about any of it – the town, my life, such as it was, my future, such as it wasn't – except her. I tried to get Abby to look at me. She did, sort of. She kept one eye on the street corner. I wanted to say something meaningful.

"Abby…"

"Okay, whatever you say," she said. "We'll find each other someday. Maybe. Just, just go and don't look back. Never."

She meant it. She was cold. This wouldn't be a precious

moment. She eased me onto the truck seat, scanning the corner for oncoming headlights. When I was in, she stepped away. I reached for the door and closed it halfway. And then I knew I did want to go. I had broken all the rules in that town, as near as I could tell. It was time for something new. I pictured myself at the wheel, the road coming at my windshield, and all this fading away. But there was a problem. I didn't want to go alone. I didn't want the music to stop. I hurled the door back open and stepped out.

"Go with me."

"Oh, for God's sake, Matt."

"I can take care of you. Of us."

I think I actually believed that, at least right then. Abby screamed and started beating on me. I tried to dodge her fists and grab her arms at the same time. She couldn't be contained. Lights came on in the neighboring houses.

"Take care of me?" Now the whole block could hear. "You can't take care of yourself."

I could feel the stubborn boiling up in me. It wasn't about her. The stubborn was never specific. It was just stubborn. I pushed her away. Too hard. She tumbled backward onto the grass. Hard. It astonished me. I came toward her.

"I'm sorry. Sorry."

Everything was different now. I could tell she wasn't hurt. She never took her eyes off the corner. All I wanted was to see her back up. Standing. I bent. I gestured. Helpless. Stupid.

"I didn't mean to...here, let me...I'm sorry. Please."

She waved me off.

"Go, you fool. Go. I don't want you here. Go and grow up on somebody else's time." I knelt down and tried to kiss her.

"Go, damn you."

While I was trying to recall if she'd ever used a swear word before, she stood up. She eyed me, hard.

"You're a self-centered, irresponsible child in a man's body. I don't want you. Nobody wants you. Even your parents…"

She stopped. I guess she thought this would hurt me. It didn't. I was almost nineteen. My parents didn't so much leave me, they just got out as early as they could. Not that I blamed them. They did all the right things. I rewarded them by doing all the wrong ones. They left me their address. It was somewhere on the floor inside.

She slumped. The hard vanished. I rose. Our faces almost touched.

"Oh, God. Matt. I'm sorry. Sorry. But, but it's true. This town is a bridge, and you burned it."

She was usually more original than that. I reached out to embrace her. She backed away, trembling. You could tell she was determined.

"Matt. I swear, even if you stay, you will never see me, you will never touch me again. Never."

There isn't much distance between stubborn and angry. I crossed it. I turned my back on her, got in the truck, and started it. Time for the last word.

"Then burn the portrait, too."

I revved the motor.

Abby came to the window and touched my arm.

"Don't turn your lights on until you get around the corner."

That was Abby. She got the last word, and it was a kind one.

I floored it, and the old truck lurched away with a juvenile screech. If I had looked back, I would have seen Abby, wrenched and agonized, watching me escape around the corner just before a pair of headlights emerged from the opposite direction. I

9

would have seen that for a moment, she just stood there, holding on to nothing, before shivering into sobs.

If I had looked back, I know I would have turned around. Maybe.

✳✳✳

I drove angry. I delivered a soliloquy to the windshield: "Child. Self-centered. Oh, for God's sake, Matt." I thought the impression was pretty good.

I slapped the wheel and let out all the swear words I knew. There aren't that many. It helped. Now, I could just relax and mutter, except I couldn't relax.

Main street widened, and storefronts right and left came and went. The high school passed my window. I gave it the finger. Then houses, the nice ones fronting the main road. Then the farm implement dealer and our only hamburger stand and the grain towers, and then it was over.

Soon I was moving too fast through a cornstalk canyon. One of those one-lane blacktops with no fencerow or ditch to speak of. When the corn was high, there wasn't a day in Nebraska when the horizon was visible.

And then there it was, the two-lane. Stripe down the middle. I stopped. The truck calmed down. I got out and slammed the door and kicked the ground and left the truck idling and walked to the stripe. There was no traffic. You could lie down and sleep on that road this time of night.

I could feel the squall in my chest passing. I pulled my smokes from the sleeve of my t-shirt, then rolled the pack back in. I lit one. Big drag. I glanced at the moon. I felt stupid. Big exhale.

"Which way ya gonna go, kiddo?"

Now there was a surprise. I wasn't alone. I turned toward the voice. It wasn't just any voice. You have to drink a lot of whiskey and burn a lot of cigarettes to get a voice like that. You could sand firewood with it. But there was also an odd hint of melody. Impish.

"Kiddo," I said. It wasn't an invitation to a chat.

He was reclining on a duffel bag. He stuck his thumb up and made the hitchhiker motion. Lazy. You couldn't get more casual. He was older than me – jean jacket, boots, a formless fedora from God knows when – but I couldn't tell much else. There was no color to him in the moonlight. Just grays and blacks. The fedora shaded his face. If he hadn't spoken, I would never have noticed him.

I didn't answer the gesture. I wasn't looking for new friends. But it was a good question and it was still in the air. I looked east. I looked west. I didn't look back. I pulled a coin from my pocket – the biggest one, a fifty-cent piece. We used those back then. I flipped it. The coin landed at my feet. Heads.

"East," I said.

"Not my way," he said.

This worked out since I wasn't offering a lift.

"But I do smoke," he said.

I pulled out my smokes, took one and stuck it behind my ear. I dropped the pack next to the coin at my feet. I wasn't normally so unselfish, but I had a carton in the truck. Also, I didn't feel like bending over. And, well, there was something about the guy. I made for the truck. By the time I slid in and looked back through my windshield, the hitchhiker was standing on the stripe, cigarette lit. He held up the coin between two fingers and turned it back and forth before his still darkened face like a prize. He spoke to himself, but loud enough to hear over the motor.

"There's a third direction."

I leaned out my door window. The truck motor died. The breeze faded. Silence crowded in. Can a late summer night in a sea of Nebraska corn feel claustrophobic? Yes.

I did what I always did when I felt cornered. I pulled the cigarette from behind my ear and slid it between my lips. Ever so casual. Flipped my Zippo open, flicked the flint, swept the flame just so, and snapped the cap. Big healthy drag. A masterful demonstration of a useless skill. Even I knew it was theater.

I looked over what I could see of him. Formless. I could feel him eyeing me from under that hat brim. Whether I liked it or not, I would hear about the third direction. I did.

"You could go back."

This stopped me mid-drag. I actually thought about it. I could picture it – me getting out of the truck and taking on those boys and winning and then facing the old man. Abby all the while trying to get in the middle of it. And then, no. I let it go. All of it. It was easy to let go. Surprisingly easy. Too easy. I gave the hitchhiker my give-a-damn look and blew the smoke.

"East," I said.

I fired up the truck and pulled onto the two-lane and eased it left. The hitchhiker stayed on the center stripe, so I had to angle around him. He neared my window. He was an arm's length away and still colorless. In the light, I could only see his mouth and chin. He had what you call "no distinguishing features." Three-day stubble. A haircut he self-delivered poking from under the hat. Somewhere behind the shadow of the brim, you knew he had that one-eyed cigarette squint going. He took a drag, and the glow lit up his lips, which crooked into something like a smile.

I didn't like it.

"East," he said. "I guess that's where the trouble ain't."

Now, I was too close to him. He didn't move. I braked before I clutched. The truck died. What did that mean? What did he know? How could he know? I gave him my you-ain't-that-smart look.

"Hey," he said. He glanced into the truck bed and shrugged. "You, here, hustling away in the dark. I guess any direction is better than back."

I restarted the engine.

"Back off," I said.

The hitchhiker gave me some room. I pulled away.

"See ya 'round, kiddo."

You wonder why people waste words. As I drove away into the night, I caught myself in the rearview mirror. The smear of red was still on my cheek.

Abby.

I never told her I loved her. Ever.

✳✳✳

After a few miles, I slowed down. I stayed on the two-lane, driving east and south. I still don't know how long. One small town after another rolled up and vanished. More hours passed.

The predawn, then full gray. Lights flickered on in the little stores and houses and I knew each had a story, and I also knew I didn't give a damn what they were.

Then, sun. It should have made me feel better. It didn't.

I rolled. Hours passed.

Kansas City surprised me. How did I get there that fast? I wouldn't stop. Didn't want to stop. Too much city. Suddenly, everybody wanted to go where I was going, at least for the moment.

"So, this is rush hour."

I said it aloud. I knew the term. I'd just never seen one, much less been in one. How do they live this way, all jammed up? I decided to enjoy it. They were in a hurry. I wasn't. Maybe I could get in the way and piss a few people off. My day started badly. Why not theirs? There was one lane, then two. They filled gradually. Then a dam burst. No, it was a stampede. Cars and trucks swelling in my mirror. Rising headlong. Then swerving by. Rushing noise. Maybe that's where the name comes from.

I leaned back. Elbow on the window. Arm draped over the wheel. Cigarette dangling. I drove slowly and let them flow over me. They honked, annoyed. Well, good. As we crossed the Missouri River, I decided to be unimpressed by the swagger of the cityscape, which was actually impressive.

Everybody had a purpose but me. They peeled off and steered into the swagger and became part of the cityscape. Again and again and again. And then the rush was gone. It was like being in a canoe and leaving the rapids behind.

And like that, my windshield was full of empty, except for concrete and grass. They were constructing a four-lane highway into the city from the other side, too. The Missouri side. Now that the cars were gone, you could take it all in.

Like most people at that time, I'd never seen a highway like this. I tried it for a while and got off. There was something too clean and too loud about it.

Also, my truck didn't like moving that fast.

I stayed on the back roads after that, the old paved ones –

too small for a stripe in the middle. The cool of the night was gone. I opened up the cigarette vents on the doors, and the morning air blew through my shirt from both directions. It should have felt better.

I pulled into a roadside store and got gas and a case of beer and a bunch of those little white donuts. Now, along with my cigarettes, I had three of the food groups. The store was one of those one-room, wood-floored places that died off one by one as the highway construction inched forward and passed them into oblivion. I wasn't old enough to buy beer legally, but I could pull it off. I'd learned it's easier in the morning. I don't know why.

The guy in the store eyed me up and down. There wasn't much to him. He'd spent so much time in that room he looked like part of the room. Why do skinny guys wear suspenders? The place was old school. No reach-in coolers. You had to ask him for what you wanted, and he put it on the counter, so I asked and gave him my you-really-don't-want-to-cross-me look. He rang me up. When you look like trouble, I think they just want to get you out of the place before you start any.

I'd always looked like trouble. Hell, I *was* trouble, but today, I didn't want any, and that was a new feeling.

Back to the truck. I shoved myself into the cab. Huge exhale. I was tired of trouble. I was tired of myself. Or maybe I was just tired. I sat there, not wanting to answer for anything.

I don't know how long I sat in the mid-morning still. Except for the slow swelling of an approaching car now and then, it was silent. Nobody pulled in. I fiddled with the steering wheel.

You could go back.

I pictured him, the hitchhiker, saying it. He was the only human being I'd seen since this all started who was surely more worthless than me. Even Suspender Boy in the store was a better

15

man than me. Still, the hitchhiker was right. I could go back.

I tried to picture it, but I couldn't.

I swear, even if you stay you will never see me, you will never touch me again. Never.

She meant it. Or did she? Why was I doing this to myself? I'd made my decision. Or had I? I was doing the right thing, except I wasn't. I'd never done the right thing. There wasn't a right thing, anyway. Or was there?

I leaned over and grabbed the can opener that hung from my rearview mirror. I opened a beer and let the foam slide over my fingers and onto my jeans. Breakfast. I caught my eyes in the mirror. Chicken crap.

The city was way behind me. Outside my windshield and beyond the store spread door-to-door farmland. Suspender Boy kept looking out the window at me. Little, nervous peeks. It was only a matter of time before he would call whoever the authorities were in that county. I fired up the truck and headed into the farmland. Missouri in 1964. You can have any beer you want as long as it's a Bud.

When authorities saw me in those days, it charged up their cop antennae. It's like they could see the rat's nest inside my head. They would start asking questions. Where was I going? Why was I there? They would call in my description and my license number, and then it would be, "Please step out of the car."

I didn't want to do the dance with them, so I stayed on the back roads. You rarely saw a patrol car on a back road, and if you did, they weren't patrolling. They were going somewhere. They would leave me alone.

No, I didn't want to answer for anything. I wanted to drive away and drain my can of breakfast in peace. I wanted my mind to stop. I drove nice and slow. Farms came and went. I passed a stubby tractor – one of those wide-bodied, workhorse Fords – pulling a flatbed wagon. A little redheaded kid was driving. An old guy sat on the wagon behind him, legs dangling. He had a western hat like county sheriff's wear, and a withered old cane. They both seemed so content. I wished I had a dog.

But nice and slow didn't work any better than crazy and fast. I couldn't escape at any speed. I kept returning to that moment in the night, picturing Abby's father and brothers getting out of their truck and Abby confronting them. The boys thinking I was in the house and swearing at me, about me. Abby giving it right back. All of them going inside to see if she was hiding me. The boys kicking my stuff around, frustrated because you can't mess up a mess, then back outside, trying to force Abby into their truck while she fought them off. All the neighbor's lights flicking on. The brothers swearing at the neighbors. Abby's father in tears, confronting her. Then truck doors slamming, tires screeching, and Abby, alone once again in the street.

I wondered if the portrait survived. It was the best I ever painted, or would paint, ever. Another beer. Abby again. Her father and brothers again. Another beer, this one a little warmer.

I pictured Abby in the cab with me. She'd be relaxed. Her feet would be on the seat. She'd have some wiseacre thing to say about my driving. She'd notice things I would never see. I would feel at home right here on the road. I tossed an empty can back toward the truck bed. It missed. She would make me stop and pick it up.

I didn't. A donut and another beer.

Nebraska is flat-flat. The central Missouri prairie is flat, but it also has a roll to it. But both places had corn and plenty of it. So, it was easy and familiar. You could lose yourself out in the open, and I did, or at least tried to. More farms. Little

17

clusters of houses and barns. Laundry on the line. Antique farm implements rusting in the grass. Now and then, a horse. It was green for August. Must have been a wet summer. You could smell it. Earthy, with a hint of decay. I drove. I wanted more road behind me than ahead of me.

I stuck to the paved roads, making turns for no particular reason and generally heading east. At least it was a direction. If you aren't going anywhere, you can't get lost. There was a rhythm to it. It repeated itself – drive, smoke, donut, drive, drink, stop, take a leak, drive, smoke, donut, drive, drink, stop, take a leak, and add some oil, which the pickup burned in quarts.

The day passed. It didn't get better. Every little crossroads rolled up like a promise and died on arrival. I needed music, but wherever I was wasn't anywhere. I couldn't even get preaching on the radio.

And then I stopped. There was a yellow detour sign propped up in the road. How could there be a detour? This *was* a detour. The arrow pointed down a gravel road. I didn't want gravel. My tires were bald. But I didn't want to turn around.

The sun was setting behind me. The color was high and deep and sweeping as only prairie sunsets can be. It marched toward you and away from you at the same time. You could almost hear it. The colors. Sky blue pink. You could try to paint it, but you'd never nail it. It was something real that would look phony on canvas. This was a good place for a cigarette. I realized my mind had finally stopped, which started it up again.

Abby. Another hot beer.

You could go back.

How far was it now? The day and morning and night jumbled and sifted through what was left of my brain. The calculations kept shifting. If I turned around, I could be at Abby's

18

by tomorrow morning if I didn't sleep. Or was it by noon? I could sleep in the truck. How far was it, again? What if I took the main highways? Okay, by tomorrow night, about supper time. I could see myself at her door. She'd be astonished and grateful and loving. Or not. We'd make something at my place. I don't have a kitchen. Maybe by three o'clock. Afternoons are better anyway. What about her father? Stop, dammit.

You could go back.

I'd been through this enough times. I needed to make it go away. What was it? Somewhere in the back of my head, beneath all the stupid, there it was, relentless.

There isn't going to be a baby.

So, what about it? Just another thing to pretend to forget. I had plenty of those.

It wasn't me. It was her. But it was me. I didn't care. I did care. How long had I been sitting there? Stop, dammit.

I heard a scraping, metallic sound behind me. In my door mirror, I could see the detour sign dancing in a lone gust of wind. It scraped and hopped across the road and collapsed face down in the ditch. I could picture Abby seeing the whole thing and drawling, "It's a sign." Her voice would touch just the right note of incongruity. Would any woman ever make me laugh again?

The breeze died. The grass stopped moving. The bugs went silent. Whatever it takes for a thought to start in my head, started. It formed and glued itself to other thoughts in a minuet. No, a fandango. Thoughts coming and going, gluing and ungluing until they took shape and bubbled up through the stupid. I could hear my own thought talking to me: "As far as you're concerned, what happened back there never happened. It's like you were never there."

19

Fine. I caught my face in the mirror. A glop of red. Oil paint. The last of Abby. I wiped the paint off my cheek. It was an angry swipe. Go away, Abby. I wiped my fingers on my jeans. Now, I was stained, not that I cared.

And then, somewhere in the sleepless beer haze that accounted for my brain, I pushed my last encounter with her into a place so deep even I couldn't see it. I erased her. Or maybe she erased herself. The music stopped.

I lit up the old truck and turned down the gravel road. I didn't stop to replace the sign on the road. Good citizen.

As if on cue, the sun went down.

✳✳✳

You can get lost if you need gas, which you need even if you aren't going anywhere but you still want to keep going. It was dark. Cloud cover veiled the moon. I'd been on gravel since sunset, making turns I could never retrace. I had not seen a car or a truck since I took the detour. Beer and cigarettes weren't bringing any new clarity, and the donuts were gone.

The truck sputtered and jerked and stopped. It was my gas gauge, and it muttered "empty." The other gauge, the one in the dashboard, didn't work. It had never worked. I got out and unlashed the five-gallon can I kept in the bed as a spare tank.

I hoisted the can and poured. It wasn't a clean job. I had always meant to get a spout. I poured straight from the can in the general direction of the hole. It would be an understatement to say I was unsteady. I splashed some on the truck, some on the road, some on my pants, and the rest in the tank. I tossed the can back toward the bed. It flew over the bed and into the ditch. I started to leave it there, then thought better of it.

I made my way around the bed, one hand on it for balance, and I bent over the ditch. It was black dark down there. I kicked around but couldn't feel the can in the brambles. I nosed in and pushed the weeds and sticks aside. Now, it was blacker than black. My body kept moving downwards and blood rushed to my head like I was falling into a hollow. I felt like I was being engulfed by the ditch. My hands thrashed and shoved and grabbed. Frantic. And then I nabbed the can.

I arose dizzy and stumbled back into the tailgate. I slid down. I knew the bumper would catch me, and I could sit there and regroup. It didn't. I hit the gravel. My head hit the bumper. I knew it would hurt tomorrow. Or was this already tomorrow?

The ground moved. Dizzy again, only worse. I sat there and regrouped. Had I been out? There wasn't a sound out there. Something had changed. It was dark earlier. Now it was black. I couldn't see a reflection in any direction. I couldn't see anything, only more blackness. I pulled myself upright and traced the truck bed with my hands – part braille, part crutch – back into the cab. In the dark, it felt like returning home.

I was too loose and jangly. The smart thing would have been to stay and sleep it off, so I started up the truck and moved on. There weren't any stars. The dark was oppressive. My headlights carved a triangle in the black. I switched on my brights, and the triangle got bigger, which just made the black seem bigger.

After a while – I don't know how long – I dug out a map. I knew this was pointless. It was a regional map of midwestern America, but it was the only map I had. It was in the glove box when I bought the truck. I unfolded the thing and squinted through cigarette smoke and my dash lights while I steered with my knees and spilled beer and ashed on my shirt. Damned if I wasn't right. It was pointless. The map did not show one-lane county roads in central Missouri. It did show Oklahoma and Iowa, so I knew I wasn't lost. Bacon and eggs sounded real good.

I entered a long curve. Light. The fencerow in my right window appeared and disappeared. I looked above the map and out the window. More light. You could see shapes. They took form. There were a couple of buildings centered beneath trees in a large open yard. Near the edge of the yard was a fenced-in square. There was a telephone pole with a light on it. I watched it pass, then felt a thump. The truck lurched.

I had my right front wheel in the ditch. I yanked the steering wheel hard left, which drove the right rear wheel into the ditch just in time to point the front end of the truck directly at a culvert. I stiff-armed the dash with both arms before I hit. Hard.

I don't know if the cigarette dropped from my lips before or after the dash drove my arms backward, my face hit the steering wheel, and the shifter rose up from the floor and rammed into my side. I felt a crunching sound at my feet. Then, the motor was silent. I looked down through the steering wheel. My pants were on fire. The gasoline. First one leg, then the other. Odd, the flames started small and green, then blue, then poofed into big orange ones. I stared at them. It seemed like a long time. My ears were ringing. Loud. I wanted to tell somebody about the colors. I was in pain, but I couldn't tell where. I was glad I didn't have a dog. There was yelling. Someone was talking to me. My door fell away. There were hands on my shoulders. They pulled me out onto the road. I landed hard. Someone was wrapping my legs. The fire went away. I stared into the black.

My nose and right ankle and left pinky were broken, and I had two cracked ribs and a dislocated shoulder. I lost some teeth. My legs were burned below the knee. The old truck would never run again.

It was the best thing that ever happened to me.

II

DAY ONE

SIXTEEN YEARS LATER

D ad."
I knew the voice.

"Dad."

The voice shivered with excitement. I felt a poke on my shoulder.

"Dad."

Another poke. I opened and closed one eye. What I saw was either a talking dandelion or my daughter. I opened again. Daughter. Her little face inches from mine, flushed and bug-eyed. Her nebula of white hair blocked out the skyline, or in this case, the room line.

"Dad. It's snowing."

She delivered the news and rushed off. Thump, thump, thump, thump fading down the hall. I closed my eye. I knew things would fade to black again.

One minute more. One precious minute.

I felt my hands relaxing. The rest would follow.

Thump, thump, thump, thump growing louder into the room. Another poke.

"Dad."

Could the voice be more excited? Yes. I opened one eye.

"Dad. It's snowing in the backyard, too."

And she was gone. Is a minute of sleep worth becoming the lead headline in the Bad Father News? Yes. Okay, no. I pushed myself up and sat on the edge of the bed and stared at my feet.

"Just look at your hair."

I knew the voice.

"Matt."

Hearing her call my name enveloped me with affection, but there was something else in the voice. An assignment from headquarters. I looked up. My wife was offering me a baby. A mid-size model that looked familiar. I accepted it and my wife was gone. I sat there and looked at my feet and the baby on my lap looked at me. He grabbed my nose. I had my first coffee thought. He pulled at my nose. Strong. I let my neck go loose. The baby turned my head toward him. We looked at each other. He turned it back, in full control now. He turned it up, down and in a sort of circle until my head was back where it started. I was deeply happy. Coffee thought number two.

I looked past him at the photographs framed on my nightstand. A big one and a little one. The little one was of the Reverend Gray Jarvis and me, fifteen years ago, a week or so before I got rid of my Chicago Boxcar hair for good. It never looked right with overalls. In the photo, Gray and I stood before a gazebo. You could tell it was new. I held a hammer like a trophy. We were beaming. The word "Grace" was chiseled into the beam over the entrance.

Gray Jarvis – preacher, janitor, groundskeeper, gardener, and counselor for a grateful congregation. The man who pulled me from a dying truck and smothered the flames so many years ago. The man who brought me peace. He says I brought it to myself.

We disagree.

The larger photo showed my parents in one of those formal portraits people get. The pose – he standing, she seated – a little wooden, actually very stiff, but real. Gray found my parents and brought them to me. He introduced them to the son they always wanted. They became the wonderful grandparents they always wanted to be. I looked at these two pictures every day. Often.

Time to stand. I did, and the little family of Matt and Jill Andrews – starring baby Mitt and enthusiastic weather girl Annie – was now vertical and the day could begin. A robe donned one-handed was my closing move. Coffee thought number three, this time provoked by a scent from downstairs.

At the bottom of the stairs Jill awaited with a cup of coffee in one hand. A pair of snow boots dangled from the other. This continued her long tradition of trying to hand me things when my hands were already full.

I gave her my look that said, "Notice my hands are full."

She gave me her look that said, "Not my problem."

I corkscrewed Mitt to the floor. Nobody makes better airplane sounds than me. I arose and accepted the coffee with both hands.

I gave her my look that said, "Notice my hands are still full."

Jill put the boots on the floor.

It didn't snow very often in Atlanta. It was checkmate when it did. No one moved. A city where snowfalls are rare doesn't invest much in snow removal. The stuff would melt before a plow got to us. We had a shovel, somewhere. Probably near the sled.

They say you should always start the day with a good breakfast, so I had more coffee. I faked being distracted by it. It didn't work – Jill didn't go looking for the shovel. Annie emerged. At least I thought it was her. It was a pair of arms around a pile of winter clothes with little legs below and dandelion hair above. Gloves and hats and scarves falling to the floor. She let all the clothes go and sat in the pile and mobilized her gear. When you're three and a half and it's snowing, you put your boots on before your pants.

I took my coffee and left Jill in charge and managed a one-hand ransack of the hall closet. Slow and steady. As little bending over as possible. It was morning. Coat first. Coffee. To the back-hall closet. Coffee. Shovel. Unfortunately, it was there.

✳✳✳

Midtown Atlanta in 1980 was block upon block of conventional, middle class neighborhoods populated by young people who did not consider themselves conventional or middle class. The streets were quiet and safe and long and straight. Big trees. Older homes. Porches. You could walk downtown from there.

It was pretty in the snow, but everything is pretty in the snow, except parking lots. I shoveled the sidewalk. Annie and I rolled up a conventional, middle class snowman. Hat, scarf, the whole deal. I demonstrated an excellent snow angel. Annie made a lesser twin. She was now fully introduced to snow. She wasn't interested in any snow martial arts. No fort. No snowball ammo. She busied herself with the snow. More of an abstract expressionist approach. I looked up. Jill was at the window, Mitt on her arm. Could I get more content? No.

And like that, I returned to the moment in the delivery room when the doc lifted Annie and changed every fiber of my being. For one, I expected a boy. Even at that, the whole idea of a baby was an abstraction. Other people had babies. Annie made it real, just by showing up.

Before that moment, I thought I had found my genuine worth many years before in a rural Missouri county. It was simple enough. All I had to do then was stop being the person I was, and the Reverend Gray Jarvis was there to help me pull it off. But first, he had to pull me out of a burning truck. There was a magic to him. He made it easy. He made me want to do it.

That day at the hospital was different. I instantly knew and understood a better and far more fulfilling purpose. Annie was ours and we were hers. From that moment on I was her father, and I understood exactly what that meant. I didn't need any help. It was all so clear. I was, at last, who I was born to be. It was instinct and it was there and fully formed in an instant. It was the easiest thing I ever did.

Now Jill was at the door. Another message from headquarters.

"Are we going to make a living today?"

This was the nudge-and-trudge. She nudges me out of the house. I trudge to work. My wife. My dance partner. She believes in me. She believes in me more than I do. She makes me laugh. You can't measure that.

I love my work. I'm really good at it. It makes me feel good at the end of the day. But I hate it when work gets in the way of a good time. I looked down at Annie, fully immersed in the snow. The father instinct kicked in. I gave our current condition about a minute and a half more. That's when she would go from heedless, high-octane bliss to soggy, chilled, take-me-inside-

29

now misery. Time to call it a morning. I delivered Annie to the kitchen to thaw and nabbed a briefcase and a traveler coffee. Work. I walked downtown through the snow and got there more or less on time.

✳✳✳

I slapped through the entrance of the South's Most Important Newspaper and stamped off the snow and approached Helen The Receptionist, the guardian of the door. Helen was near retirement. Helen had been to Hawaii. Other than Atlanta, it was the only place Helen had ever been. She pronounced the state name with a "v" – Havaii. You knew Helen had been to Havaii because she worked it into every conversation.

"Well, I guess winter's here," I said.

"Are the street's still slick?" she asked.

"Here and there," I said.

"When I was in Havaii – that's the correct pronunciation – the streets weren't slick, even in the heavy rain."

I gave her my you-speak-the-truth nod and made for the elevator and the vertical alignment of newspaper persona types. It was seven floors. The top floor was the executive suite. The next floor, number six, was the editorial department. Below that were two newsroom floors, The Journal on the fifth floor, The Constitution on four. Everything below was advertising and circulation, which was a handy arrangement because that way the newsroom reporters and editors could look down on them. The lower floors were engaged in the crass activity of making money and paying the salaries on the floors above them. Underneath it all, in a windowless basement, was production, where the paper was assembled and printed.

I pushed the button for Sixth Floor, Editorial, to resume my duties as the most loathed person in the newsrooms below.

But first, The Morning Gauntlet.

E. Farley Haman awaited me outside my office. He just happened to be there, like every morning. Tall and bony and longing for an aura of authority.

"You again missed the morning consensus conversation," he said.

"Again missed," I said.

Newspaper editorial writers come in three versions. Those who drone, those who dissemble, and those who seethe. When he wasn't droning, E. Farley Haman seethed. Injustice was sewn into every seam and fiber of the fabric of public life, and nature had appointed E. Farley Haman to unravel it all. He knew this in a place deep inside himself, a place too deep for tears. Every day he bent over his keyboard. Every day forests were felled, pulp mills stunk up whole counties, paper rolled through the press and whole tanker trucks of ink were drained in service of his quest.

The next day, everything was still unjust. Worse, you could look out the window and see the people happily going through their lives, unmoved by the cerebrations of E. Farley Haman. They could not see! No, they chose not to see! No, a cabal of the forces of greed coerced them to look the other way!

There, under the cover of faculty chambray and corduroy, he seethed. I walked past him, and almost made it into my office.

"I have an idea I want you to draw out," he said.

Here is how it was supposed to work. I was the editorial cartoonist – the young editorial cartoonist. I was part of the editorial department, which consisted of five writers and Haman, the editorial page editor. In a typical situation, he and the writers

31

gathered in the morning to decide what the official position of the paper would be on the day's topics. Then Haman would assign a writer to a topic. The cartoonist may or may not be a part of this. Haman wanted me to be a part of it. Always.

Also, this was Monday. Haman considered the Monday meeting vital. Make that super vital. I don't know why. I feared asking.

The Morning Consensus Conversation wasn't a consensus and it wasn't a conversation. It was an hour in the stockade listening to Haman tell you what you thought. It did occur in the morning, that much was accurate. I attended two of these meetings at one time – my first and my last.

In a typical situation, Haman would be my boss. Mine wasn't a typical situation. Seven years earlier, Gray mailed some of my cartoons to the publisher of the newspaper, a seventh-floor guy who Gray knew from the Navy. The publisher brought me to Atlanta and hired me without telling anyone, including E. Farley Haman, who never forgave him or me and never stopped yearning to control me, which is why I turned away from him at the door and gave him my we've-both-been-here-already look.

"No, Farley."

"Dr. Haman."

Did I mention he had a PhD?

"I'm not your student. And no, just like yesterday and the day before and the day before. No."

"I am the editorial page editor, your commanding officer."

Did I mention that Haman saw combat in Vietnam? He was almost as good as Helen the Receptionist at working this resume bullet into every conversation.

"I know, and do you know what that means? It means you are not the publisher. I'm gonna draw what I'm gonna draw. And

32

I'm not coming to your stupid meeting. You and your consensus bullsh…"

I stopped myself, or more precisely, a Gray Jarvis moment stopped me.

Gray and I were tending the yard of an aging parishioner. I was handling a hoe, which I had just managed to bury in a toe. Gray waited for the flash of invective to pass, and as he so often did, chose that moment to allow me take stock of myself.

"The word gracious can be interpreted as 'grace-filled.' To be filled with grace allows us to engage the world in such a way that we face the good. Are you grace-filled, Matt? Are you gracious, or are you a work in progress?"

As usual with Gray, the moment had nothing to do with the hoe. Also, as usual with Gray, I understood his question to contain the answer. I was, then and now, a work in progress. The Chicago Boxcar I could cut off. My vocabulary, that was still part of the progress. And now, years later, I had learned to control it, but only enough to chop off half a word. At least it was the vulgar half, so I called that progress.

Haman bulled up on me. He tried to flex. Did I mention we both went to the same gym every day? His face went red, starting just above his bow tie and creeping up to eye level. I could do that to him.

"Nobody here agrees with you," he said. "Ever."

"We done here?" I said, "Or is this the part where you call me a Nazi?"

"I hate that I am forced to publish your execrable cartoons," he said. "And you can't draw the human form."

This was true. I couldn't draw the human form. It was also true, and still is, that it is impossible to offend me. Years before, Gray forced me to confront the truth about myself – the good

33

and the bad – and accept it. Once you have done that, you cannot be offended. What is said about you is either true, in which case you already know it, or it is not true, and you already know that, too. If it isn't true, well, that's their problem. This was another Gray Jarvis lesson. The world will figure you out sooner or later and there is nothing you can do about it.

"Execrable," I said. "I need to look that up."

"I know the difference between you and me. You aren't a team player."

I ever so gently grasped the door and gave him my this-is-important-news look.

"The difference between you and me is that nobody ever wanted to be you."

The redness reached his hairline, which was way up there. Actually, it was more of a magenta. Hint of purple.

He took a step toward me. Remarkable, really, how he managed to look permanently offended. I knew that someday I'd ask him about that.

I gently closed the door. Exhale. Being gracious, I'd get to that, but now it was to work.

I already knew what I would draw. This wasn't always the case, but it was the first month of a presidential election year. For cartoonists, every day is your birthday in election years. There's a new gift waiting when you wake up, and somehow, it's just what you always wanted.

I fired up my coffee pot. This violated an E. Farley Haman rule. He operated a communal pot near his office, affording him opportunities to arrest you and tell you what you think. Make that, tell you again.

In minutes, I had pencil in hand before a cleared drawing table. In no time, I was in the drawing zone.

Entering the drawing zone is like pulling the cord on a reverse lamp. All the lights go out except the one over your table. Nothing enters the drawing zone without your permission. Anything that wants in has to wait in line. You could have a sprained ankle, a death in the family, and an eviction summons – all at the same time – and it wouldn't matter. Time stops in the drawing zone, even when you're on deadline. After a few years in the newspaper business, deadlines get built into you. I couldn't draw slow if I had to.

When I came out of the zone, I checked the clock. I had the cartoon penciled. Plenty of time to ink the thing and get it down to Poddy and the boys in engraving, the production department that rendered drawings printable. There was no color on editorial pages in those days. Only pen and ink. The ink was black. You could pick the pen. My pencil lines were loose. Mostly they were guidelines. I inked it tight. I was still doing Modigliani.

And then it was time to step back and take it in. When it left my desk it had to be an Andrews. It was. I called a copyboy and the thing was off to Poddy. I didn't make a copy. Many cartoonists keep a separate drawer to store Pulitzer material, but I didn't bother. The Pulitzer would never go to a guy who thinks like me.

I didn't care. Like I said, I was good – very good – at my job. I knew it and that was enough. Another Gray Jarvis lesson.

The 1980 presidential election would be a contest between an actor from California and a preachy incumbent from Georgia. The actor wasn't the nominee yet, but I was already behind him. This did not make me popular in the Atlanta newsroom.

During his term in office, the President's home state newspaper becomes one of the most important papers in the country, circulated on the streets of Washington, D.C. We were that newspaper.

Important figures – or figures who considered themselves important – yearned for access to the op-ed pages of Important Newspapers. In those days, when you opened a folded paper to the back of the first section, the editorial page was on the left. The newspaper expressed its positions there. On the right – the opposing page, or op-ed – was space reserved for other opinions. If you were a politician or a pundit and couldn't get access to the Washington Post or New York Times, our paper was third in line.

This was catnip for Dr. E. Farley Haman. At the communal coffee pot, he'd casually impart that he'd just gotten off the line with the Minister of Transportation in Luxembourg, or somebody. If the preachy Georgian lost the White House, Farley's phone would go dead again.

But my politics did make me popular out there in reader-land, where the subscribers roam. The incumbent President was doing a lousy job and all the preaching and cooked-up alibis on the planet couldn't hide it. My cartoons generated hate mail and love notes and plenty of both. Poor old Farley received a correction from a bureaucrat now and then, but that was about it. That's tough for a guy who believes in his soul that every reader devours his every word.

Worse yet, they used my 'toons and my image in marketing campaigns. Love me or hate me, I was reason alone to buy a copy. I sold papers. The seventh-floor guys knew that, and so did floors one to three. And, sadly for him, so did Farley. The attaboys just weren't there for him. It was another reason to seethe.

✳✳✳

I don't, as they say, "do lunch," unless I have to, which is rare. It felt like a rare day. I skipped the gym and walked toward my diner. The Morning Gauntlet had been particularly rough and I didn't feel like confronting E. Farley Haman in my skivvies. Also, I wanted to reread The Letter.

I hadn't yet told Jill about The Letter. I couldn't find the right words to explain it. It was a sure thing that wasn't a sure thing. One of the Big Five syndicates was sending a team of execs to meet me the next day. That was the sure thing. I knew they weren't flying from Kansas City just to see how I parted my hair. They were ready to offer me a contract, and I would surely sign it.

From there, it wasn't a sure thing. A syndicate contract was a shot at a national audience. It was only a shot, but with one of the Big Five, it's the best shot you can get. They would package my work and pitch it to every newspaper in the country, beginning with the big ones and working down. The sales campaign would take six weeks and it was pretty much make-or-break for me. If enough big papers bought me, the others would follow in time.

It meant money and prestige. But for me, it meant more. It meant the professional calling I found would be real.

I never replaced the easel and the bag of art supplies I left on the curb that night in Nebraska. I never wanted to. Painting was part of the life I left behind. When Gray took me in, I became his assistant handyman, although he prettied up the position by giving me the title of "sexton." The pay was room and board and a pack of gum. I couldn't afford canvas and paint and brushes, but I didn't care. Picking up a brush just didn't feel right.

I worked in Gray's churchyard for two years before I enlisted

37

and did my tour in the Navy.

Gray was in the Navy, and he said that's where the smart people were.

I spent most of my tour in Norfolk, Virginia, before shipping off to Spain. I sent sketches back to Gray instead of letters. I could write okay, but I could say it better with a drawing. Over time, the sketches turned into cartoons. By the time I came back, I had a style. If you're a cartoonist, or you want to be one, your style is half of everything. You want to be able to pin up your drawing on a wall alongside the work of a hundred others and see that yours is distinct. And repeatable.

After my tour, I went back to the churchyard with a style but nothing to say. I was 22. Gray suggested college. I lasted a semester, and only that long because Gray paid for it. A college campus in 1969 was the center of stupid. Way too many people with nothing to say and a craving to say it.

It was suspended reality. Boys looked like skinny lumberjacks from the neck down and one of the Twelve Apostles from the neck up. Apostles or not, they still ogled girls – girls in long homespun dresses who looked like they should be following a Conestoga wagon. Parallel fantasies.

The lumberjack Apostle boys and the Pioneer girls would talk late into the night about reality. The main point I could gather was that, for them, there was no such thing.

For me, it was like being in a nursery, so I quit.

I told Gray I would draw. That's what I would do. I would, I told him, figure out what to say with my drawings, and that's when Gray told me I should say what I know I believe. This was subtle. I wasn't sure I knew I believed anything, which isn't typical for a young man. He told me to write down what I thought was true about human nature, then he gave me his don't-treat-me-like-a-preacher look.

"Write down what you know about people in the here and now," he said. "It will be a road map for everything else."

I began with one of the first lessons he taught me: there isn't an eighth Deadly Sin.

Gray and I spent my second summer at the church constructing a gazebo. He'd always wanted to build it. He had drawn his own blueprint and kept it in an old file drawer in his office. He called it his "orison bower." He said maybe my unlucky moment with the truck was his lucky moment with the gazebo. I had fairly accomplished construction skills – it's not like I didn't work in Nebraska.

I didn't know Gray planned to use our time together as an outdoor classroom. The gazebo was an octagon. As we built it, Gray had me carve the Seven Deadly Sins – Pride, Greed, Lust, Envy, Gluttony, Wrath, and Sloth – on the top boards of seven of the sides. He talked about each of them as I went. He expounded on Aristotle, Aquinas, Dante, Plato, Descartes, Ben Franklin, Mark Twain, Solomon, and the Books of Proverbs and Ecclesiastes in no particular order and sometimes all at once. He talked about the way these seven sins stand between a man and his better side.

But he didn't call them sins. "These do not represent evil," he said. "They represent the absence of good. They are what make you human and are also what keep you from being fully human."

Somehow, I kept up. It was more or less familiar territory. Up until then, I had been guilty of most of the sins, most of the time.

On the eighth board, over the entrance, he had me carve 'Grace,' and explained, "The seven deadly sins are natural. They come from nature. Human nature. Grace is supernatural and so are its expressions – faith, hope, and charity. I will leave you with this. You must find your own way to grace. I cannot guide you."

And the gazebo, along with my lesson, was complete.

Or so I thought. That summer turned out to be the beginning of my education. Now that I had quit college and was back in the churchyard – back home – Gray would continue it. He had a pleasant, sunlit office in a corner room of the first floor of his house. You could see the whole little churchyard spread from there – church, graveyard, outbuildings, garden, gazebo, and a little pond. The prairie view was hedged in by trees. There, he taught me to read. Oh, I knew how to read letters, words and sentences. I just didn't know how to connect them with their larger purpose. I also didn't know what to read. Gray did.

An endless caravan of books came my way – literature, history, philosophy. We worked one-on-one in that sunlit room. He made me chew over what I had read. He questioned me. I did most of the talking. When Gray did speak, he had a little baton, like symphony conductors use, and he described patterns in the air. He never offered answers. Only questions. Answers, he told me, are for experts who know only what is already known. Let them have their well-trod past. Only questions are alive. It was ruthless and grueling and wonderful.

Years went by. I hardly noticed. Then the day came that Gray said it was time for my graduation ceremony. He produced a roll of cellophane from his drawer. I gave him my okay-now-what look. He waved the roll in the air like a baton.

"From now on," he told me, "you want to avoid the easy way of looking at things. Everybody has a point of view about the big things – life, the world, all of it. You can, if you want, arrive at your point of view early and spend the rest of your life clinging to it, acknowledging the evidence – and only that evidence – that

40

verifies it."

He told me to stick out my hands, like for a cat's cradle, and he wrapped the cellophane around them once. It was comfortable and you could see through the middle, nice and clear. He wrapped them again. Not much change, but the view was a little less clear. Then again and again and again, layer upon layer until the view between my hands was distorted like a carnival mirror. I couldn't move my hands. The cellophane cinched them.. It felt suffocating, claustrophobic. I was handcuffed.

"This cellophane," he said, "behaves like the justifications and rationalizations and excuses you need in order to cling to an idea you refuse to question."

Then he told me to make a hole in the cellophane. It wasn't easy. In fact, it was painful, but eventually I tore and pushed through the layers until I got an index finger poking free. The air felt good around it. He touched my liberated finger with his baton.

"It's better out here," he said. "But it's lonely."

For the first time, he spoke to me as an equal. He was no longer my teacher. This was my graduation, which in Gray's world meant I was ready to start learning. My instruction was over. Almost.

We never talked about the final side to the gazebo, the entrance to grace. I understood that I had to figure that one out by myself.

Gray had told me I needed a road map for my work. Now, I had one. I used it, but if you asked me how, I'm not sure I could deliver a cogent reply, even though it wasn't, and isn't, complicated. There is no Eighth Deadly Sin. The virtues, too, are ancient and unchanged. People are what they've always been. In an ever-changing world, there is nothing new under the sun – a phrase I learned from Ecclesiastes – in human nature.

This didn't give me wisdom. It gave me a starting point toward it. Again and again.

Not that there aren't new things. New ideas. But falsely claiming to be something new is probably the oldest one in the books. It's breathtaking how many people buy into it. Foiling the claim is what cartoonists are born to do. My cartoons took on a new maturity. They became more perceptive, less preachy. And then, not preachy at all. I had learned to create cartoons that made people ask their own questions. Eventually, this led to Gray's letter to the Atlanta publisher. In Gray's mind, I was ready. He'd taught me to think.

Thinking. That's where most cartoonists go dry. Drawing and thinking are two very different things. You can't think in the drawing zone. You have to think before you go in. This is what the lousy cartoonists and the E. Farley Haman's of the world never get. A drawing isn't a flow chart. It doesn't read left to right like a sentence. Well, okay, that's not entirely true. A drawing can read like a sentence, but it will be a bad one. That's why you can't meet a lousy idea halfway. When somebody shoves one at you, you just have to block it until they quit trying. If you listen, you just encourage them. E. Farley Haman, a man with a remarkably narrow range of obsessions, never stopped trying.

The diner was a classic. Glass front looking into one long room. One long counter. Many stools. Hustling waitresses who called you "honey." A grill man who could conduct a symphony. If you didn't know better, you'd swear the joint had always been there, like the city had been built up around it. The thing about a diner is, everything sounds good, even if you've had it before and you know it isn't.

I knew the place. I didn't do lunch often, but I did it here. One of my cartoons was taped to the cash register. It was signed. They asked me to do it. I took a stool. The coffee came without me saying a word. The waitress asked me if I wanted a Number Five. I smiled. She called me honey and swept away.

I began reading The Letter. Actually, I just looked at the words. I'd memorized it. It just felt good. The noon rush kicked in and the diner came alive.

I was sitting on my coat. Now and then a hustling customer brushed against my back. It was all part of the scene – the press of the crowd – but each bump prompted a little golden wish for the open prairie. That would be another perk of syndication – you can live wherever you want – and I was never a city boy.

Yet another passing customer collided with me and I heard a coin fall to the floor. The customer bent over and retrieved it. I heard him place it on the counter by my hand. I glanced at the coin – a fifty-cent piece – and returned my eyes to The Letter.

I glanced at the coin again. Odd. It wasn't silver. It was black and white. There's a difference. I heard a voice.

"Ya dropped this, kiddo."

Looking back, it's hard to say. Maybe I should have recognized the voice – raspy and contrary and mocking and tuneful all at once – but, no.

"Thanks, but it isn't mine."

A hand reached over and swept up the coin. I caught the move in the corner of my eye.

Odd again. It was like the hand was in black and white and

43

the rest of the world was in color.

"I'll flip ya for it," the voice said, and I heard the ting of thumb on a coin.

I watched the coin climb in the air above me and then fall toward the counter. It seemed like it took too long. The diner went silent. The coin hit the counter with a thud and an echo, loud and muffled at the same time, like an explosion in a vacuum. It started to spin away in slow, drunken turns until I slapped my hand down on it. It was instinct, mostly. You can't watch a coin flip and not want to know how it lands.

I pulled my hand away. Tails.

And the light in my brain turned off.

III

TAILS

Odd combo. The numb and trill and tingle you get with an electric shock. I felt it across my entire body as the lights came back on to the sound of laughter – the kind they call uproarious. I mean, they were belting it out, filling the room. But it wasn't the same room. Wherever I was, it wasn't a diner.

My eyes cleared. I looked up at a large open space. High ceiling. Actually, no ceiling. Glass roof. Natural light. My new clear eyes followed my arm up to my left hand, which was holding a cigarette and a champagne flute.

A cigarette.

I looked again. My pinky finger, the broken one, wasn't crooked. My eyes swept glass above and neutral-colored walls around before lowering to the floor, only it wasn't a floor. I stood on a big square block – maybe five feet tall. It was black. I looked down on a crowd spread out around me, looking up at me. I could tell they expected something.

I hadn't held a cigarette in fifteen years. My finger had been bent for sixteen. Champagne was not my drink of choice at lunchtime. I had no clue where I was. I felt like I was spinning, like I'd survived a cyclone only to arrive in a hall of mirrors.

The laughter died down.

"Where am I?" I asked.

The people below me howled and giggled and hooted. There was a snarky quality to it. I looked them over. Urbane, stylish and arty. Black jackets, black shirts, black pants and shoes and belts and little black dresses. They all had their own champagne flutes.

I looked myself over. I was black on black, too.

The laughter faded to the titter stage. Another man in black raised his flute above the audience and toasted my feet, shouting, "That's what the critics have been asking for years!"

This one almost brought the house down. It dawned on me that, at least for the moment, I was the entertainment. They weren't laughing at me. They were laughing with me, and they wanted more. Suddenly, the room felt full of empty.

"What time is it?" I said.

That one puzzled 'em. Even so, it got a few chuckles. Not a tough room. A woman in a little black dress hoisted her flute.

"Finish your little exposition, Matthew."

Matthew. Okay at least that was right. I still had my name, even if it wasn't the version I used.

I stared at her. We'd never met. She stared back. I watched her face mudslide through three stages. What-will-he-say-next? Did-I-say-something-wrong? Is-he-okay? Then she was pushed aside.

The crowd parted, and a human torpedo homed in – hot fist in one hand, champagne flute in the other. His clothes were black and his face was crimson.

I had no clue who he was, but I could tell he was after me.

46

Usually, when I annoy someone this much, I know why. He reached the base of the square and swung one arm at my feet and ankles. I hopped away. This angered him more. He swung again. I hopped faster until I was jigging a reluctant hornpipe atop the square. The audience howled. He threw his champagne flute at me. It missed, shattering somewhere. The audience ooohed and some backed away. I used the moment to ease off the square and drop to the floor.

And there he was, steamy and snorty, his face to mine, body braced and heaving and threatening. I saw plenty of fistfights in my Chicago Boxcar days, and I knew he was all show.

I laughed, and the torpedo exploded.

"If there is a single scuff mark on Twenty-three, Sixty-nine, Five," he screamed, and it was a scream, or at least it was when he hit the high note on "single." He moved closer. "I will…"

He didn't know where to go from there. I didn't want it to go any further.

I held up my hands in the classic "I surrender" pose and then took it down to the "let's all be calm" pose. I turned toward Twenty-three, Sixty-nine, Five. There were no scuff marks, but I made a show of wiping the thing with my very expensive sleeve. I couldn't reach one place where I stood, so I put my champagne flute on the square, doused my cigarette in the flute and leaned in with both arms.

Angry Man torpedoed again. He swept the glass off the square. Another shatter. The crowd went silent. More people in black backed away.

"Twenty-three, Sixty-nine, Five is not a table, asshole."

My first thought was to ask him what Twenty-three, Sixty-nine, Five was good for, if not a table, but I held my tongue. Peace. Peace would be better, especially in a world I didn't know.

I gave it another shot. "Look, I'm sorry."

"You've ridiculed my work for the last time."

"I don't even know you."

"Bullshit. You know me and you know I know people."

People who aren't properly trained in the art shouldn't use swear words, but I let it go. Also, I didn't know I knew him, much less if he knew "people."

He pointed to a large painting on the far wall of the atrium. It had the look of an abstract, but seemed familiar somehow.

It had an audience. People lingered there, some taking notes. They turned toward our commotion, then turned back. I could see them shrug us off.

"You're a one-trick pony, Andrews. We'll see how long that thing hangs there. I know people."

Okay, so they, or at least he, had my last name right, too. I wasn't a body double. But what that thing, that painting, had do to with me I had no idea.

I must have spent too much time in thought, because when I looked back at the father of Twenty-three, Sixty-nine, Five, he was off guard. I didn't want to say anything. I was no longer sorry that I'd sullied Twenty-three, Sixty-nine, Five.

And all this black. What was it with the black clothes? If it's a matter of efficiency, I get it, but these people throw in the lipstick and the nail polish and the greasy tinted hair. Well, he didn't do the nail polish and lipstick, but his monolith was black and both it and he looked like funeral material.

He'd braced for a vicious riposte that never came. I just stood there. I wanted him to go away, and he did, after sputtering a bit and executing a sharp, military-grade, parade-ground about face.

It was time to take stock. My audience was scattered, which

was a relief. I was obviously in an art museum, and a big one. By the looks of it, this was the modern wing. A couple of bright young men with better things to do were mopping up the champagne and the broken glass and my cigarette butt.

They didn't look at me. Nobody did, which was also fine.

I took a second look at my clothes. To the extent I cared, I was embarrassed. On top of the black on black, I had that un-premeditated spread collar look that requires more time and effort than choosing and knotting a tie. When clothes are expensive, you can feel it. I wasn't dressed with cartoonist money.

Again and again, my eyes were drawn toward the canvas on the far wall, the one Angry Boy had pointed out. It was huge, a long horizontal. The audience was still there, scribbling and jotting away at their notebooks. I headed over, regarding the room along the way. I stopped a few paces behind the audience.

They were busy, these people – sketching, consulting books, and of all things, poking on calculators. I looked up to see what the fuss was about.

It wasn't an abstract canvas at all. It was realistic and relentlessly so, but it didn't just lie there dead. The thing was spiced with a pinch of impressionistic flair.

Even from behind the audience, I could tell the brushwork was remarkable. The detail was remarkable. The composition was remarkable. It was a still life. A still life of utter disarray.

And it made me very uneasy.

I knew this painting, or at least I knew about this painting. I knew a great deal of something about this painting. It kept shifting and unfolding into something familiar, like I was watching a photograph develop in the chemicals – until there it was. No mistaking it. The painting was a representation of my

49

studio floor in Nebraska all those years ago. Dead on accurate.

I did the only thing I could think to do. I pinched myself. It hurt and I was still there.

I edged around the audience toward the right of the canvas and read the title plate on the wall: Floor, 1967. Matthew Andrews. Oil on canvas.

I blew back, like a sheet on a line catching a gust of wind. I'd seen a ghost and it was me.

"Oh, my God."

The words escaped me and I must have said it loud. The audience stopped sketching and noting and calculating and turned my way. I backed farther away from the painting.

A voice came from the crowd. "Hey, it's him. It's Matthew Andrews!"

The group pressed in on me until I was surrounded. They held up their sketches and notes. They pointed to passages in books. They showed me their calculations. They asked me questions. Was what they thought to be revealed in the painting correct? What about this? What about that? Had I considered different numbers? Is this your Sistine Chapel Floor?

The questions were impossible. The only thing I knew about the painting was that I didn't paint it. I couldn't paint like that when I painted, and I still couldn't today. It was better than anything I had ever put on canvas.

I broke through the crowd and sprinted for what looked like an exit, only it wasn't. I looked back. A couple of the audience members gave chase. I ran for another exit. Wrong again. Who designs these places?

I managed to make it out of the big room, and my pursuers gave up, but I kept running out of the skylit hall, navigating the room to room circuitry until I spotted daylight. I was through the door and into daylight before I realized I'd been holding my breath. Outside! Free! It wasn't cold, which made the lack of snow both surprising and unsurprising. It's a good thing cabs are yellow. When I saw the color, I exhaled. I stopped him with a very energetic wave. I dove into the back seat.

The driver was full-time world weary. "Where to?"

"Where am I?"

My question didn't seem to surprise him. "L.A."

"What day is this?"

"Wednesday."

So far my name and the day and the country had not changed. The town was another matter.

"What number is the day? And month."

The driver squinted in the mirror.

"It's not a game show," I said. "I just need to know."

"The seventh of January."

"What year is this?"

"1980."

That one surprised him. I made the only choice I could.

"I need to go to the emergency room."

"Which one?"

"The nearest one. Wait. No, the best one."

✳✳✳

The doctor eyed me up and down from behind his clipboard. You could tell I annoyed him, and why not? I'd made what they call a commotion in the waiting room. Now I was sitting on a bed, shirtless – they always make you take your shirt off – legs dangling, surrounded by curtains. He was going over the usual

51

checklist of habits and vices and pathologies. There was a little table and a mirror on the wall. There was a nurse. She just stood there. She had an enormous bosom which was more or less acting like a table for the files in her arms, which were crossed.

"You don't smoke?" said the doc. He eyed my shirt. There was a pack of cigarettes in the pocket.

"These aren't mine. I mean, they were…"

"Have you had a cigarette today?"

"No. I mean, I don't know. Maybe. I was holding one."

"Alcohol?"

"I do drink. But it's not a big part of my life. Not anymore."

"Frequency."

"Cocktail hour. Wine with meals."

"So, every day."

I'd never thought of it that way. He was beginning to annoy me.

"Yes, I guess so."

"It isn't cocktail hour."

"There was champagne. I don't know. I was holding a glass."

"Like you were holding the cigarette?"

I didn't slug him, but I must have looked like I wanted to. The nurse shifted and took a deep bosom-swelling breath. I'm telling you, they were huge. When she moved, her nurse's badge was like a buoy in the surf. It was hard to avert the eyes. The doc got me back to business.

"Drugs?"

"The strongest thing I take is aspirin." I gave him the eye. "And I haven't had or held any today."

The nurse clutched her files tighter. A bosom lava flow.

"But I think it is maybe drugs," I said. "I think somebody gave me one of those, I don't know…something. I'm hallucinating, I think. No, I know."

"Describe them."

"Well, it's everything. I'm not supposed to be here, and neither are you."

I looked the nurse over. It dawned on me that she was blocking the way out. I was insulted. They should have sent a guy. A big one. Then again, there was the bosom.

"And neither are you," I said.

She shifted again.

"Where are you…we, supposed to be?" said the doc.

"I'm supposed to be in a lunch counter in Atlanta. I don't know where you're supposed to be."

"Atlanta?"

"I live there. With my family."

The nurse handed him one of her files. He glanced at it and snapped it on his clipboard. He shoved the board toward me and pointed to a line at the bottom. He held the board so his hands covered most of the page.

"According to this, you live here in Los Angeles. Your wife is the emergency contact. She lives at this address."

It was a local address. I was beyond surprise by then, although this should have been a big one. Time for an assessment. I looked in the mirror. It was me. Me without a broken nose. I counted the people in the mirror. Three. I pinched myself, again. It hurt, again. I considered pinching the nurse. No.

I read the address again, then memorized it.

The Letter. I slapped my pants pocket. Not there. I lunged for my jacket, or at least the jacket that I had been wearing, and jammed through the pockets. Not there. I tossed the jacket back.

Something like anger was beginning to overwhelm my confusion and fear. The nurse grew ever more nervous. When I moved, she jumped.

"He doesn't have proof of insurance." She wasn't in a goal line stance yet, but she'd planted.

"When was the last time you ate?" Asked the doc.

It wouldn't be long before the words "keep you here for observation" passed through his lips. I didn't know what to call this, but I knew enough to call it quits. I pulled the pack of smokes from my shirt pocket.

"You can't smoke here." They both said it, at exactly the same time and cadence. Remarkable.

"But they're for you." I tossed the pack at the nurse's cleavage. She dropped the files, and the cigarettes disappeared in a chasm. I was around her and beyond, shirt and jacket in hand, before she recovered. I was out the door before both of them wrestled the curtain open, and I made another fine commotion in the waiting room on the way out.

✱✱✱

When the cab pulled up to the address, it felt like a blind date. For that matter, every encounter that day had been blind. Reality wasn't batting for average.

My name and the time and date – so far, correct. The place and all the rest of it – no. If Jill answered the door, or even if she didn't, my next stop was a drink. No. Make that a shrink.

I got out and pulled my wallet, only it wasn't my wallet. It was the wallet of a man who had too much money to spend on wallets. I opened it. At least then I knew where the clothes money came from. The thing was stuffed with big number bills. I thumbed them over. North of four thousand dollars. I guess I stared at it awhile, because the driver got restless.

I kept staring. The meter was running. I didn't care.

No detail made sense, and neither did the big things. Los Angeles in real life only makes sense if you've already been there. I hadn't, so it was doubly unreal.

The city and the suburbs had passed by my window on the ride over. Apparently, there are no brief cab rides in Los Angeles. There is constant change, like we were driving from one little country to another and another. It was all there alright, but I wasn't. How could I be? I was in a diner in Atlanta.

And then it was over, the drive, I mean. Quick return to reality. I could hear the driver's fingers drumming on the dash. The money didn't matter, but I decided to play it straight.

"Can you break a hundred?"

He gave me an eyeroll, reached for a pouch under his seat and we made our exchange. I gave him a 1980 Atlanta tip. No comment either way. And then he was gone.

It looked to be an affluent neighborhood. Understated wealth and restrained taste with brushstrokes of the American Southwest and Mexico. This particular house was all curves and arches, adobe and terracotta, balconies and iron work, siennas and creams. The appointments were more unusual and artsy than what you saw on the other houses, but they fit in.

I checked the number again. Yes. Now it was down the walk and on to the door. You have to pay somebody to get grass that green in January. No cars were visible. All the garage doors were closed. It was quiet, like maybe there was a rule about that.

The door was wood, thick and heavy and weathered, like the shutters. No ringer, but there was a knocker made out of an old cowboy boot. It looked familiar. Another uppercut to the jaw. It couldn't be.

I stepped forward and traced the stitching. It was mine, or it had been mine, a long time ago. Deep breath. Slam the boot. Exhale. Wait. Deep breath. Slam the boot. Exhale. Wait. Soon enough, the door eased open.

Abby.

Instantly I heard the music. Instantly I wanted her. I firehosed it down, which made room for all the other emotions. They say you can't feel two things at the same time. If two people pinch you at once, you'll only feel one of them. Well, that may be true on the outside. In your head, that's a different matter.

Elation and fear. Affection and anguish. Desire – again – and disquiet. And beneath it all, shame. Shame beyond explanation. Shame that I left her. Shame that I wanted her. Just shame. You couldn't measure it in tons. Confusion? That was already there. It was an intoxicating, agonizing mix. I braced for an outburst.

"Since when do you knock?"

She turned and ambled back into the house, leaving the door wide open. I just stood there. Her calm drove me nuts. I always loved watching her walk. Where was that shrink I knew I needed?

She paused in the hallway. "And now you need an invitation?"

The years had been more than kind to her. She still danced between handsome and pretty, but handsome was winning. She was self-assured and graceful in her small way. Desire and affection muscled above the other emotions. Firehose again. She watched me closely and her mother look, the one I never liked, began to take shape.

"Matt. Come in."

I stepped toward her and stumbled on the sill. I went down

hard, but landed on all fours. And like that, I went empty. Weariness draped over me. I stared at the floor. Dizzy. Vacant. Hollow. You can't unpack a void. I heard Abby's feet rushing toward me. Then I saw them. Athletic shoes. Pink. I knew she had stopped, but the shoes kept moving, at least in my vision. I leaned back, on my knees before her.

"Help me."

There was a rushing sound. No, it was like voices. It may have been voices. Unintelligible cartoon voices. Low volume, speaking too fast, saying nothing, then louder, then fading. It was a surf of static, like my ears were tuned to a dozen radio stations and a child was fiddling with the knob. I could feel things going black as I dropped back down on my hands.

I wanted to go black. I wanted to black out and wake up where I belonged. But I didn't want to. I wanted to look up and see Abby again. The surf peaked, faded and didn't return. I saw her shoes stop moving. No, they were gone. She knelt beside me.

Minutes passed. At least it seemed like minutes. I could hear her asking the predictable questions. What happened? Was I alright? Was I in pain? Had I been drinking? Then her voice faded. I couldn't find mine, and responded with nods and glances, gripping her arm and delivering a big "No" when she said she was calling a doctor.

She got me back on my feet and moved me down the hall. I leaned on her. It was dark. I never took my eyes off the floor. It seemed to move by itself. Then things opened up and we entered a light filled room and I looked upward. It was like an atrium – two stories tall and windows all the way up. Abby dropped me into a couch.

For the next few minutes there was puttering and muttering. Abby fussed. I sat. I declined booze – which surprised Abby –

and asked for tea. She touched me in different ways – propping me on pillows, stroking my brow – as her mothering ways returned.

The living room was pure Abby. Straight and off kilter at the same time. My Modiglianiesque portrait survived her brothers. It was above the mantel. Do they actually use fireplaces in California?

It was a deep couch, too deep. I was folded up in it. Abby leaned forward on a chair.

The tea came. Did she deliver it? Were we alone? She examined me.

I would have felt like an exhibit, but there was warmth in her eyes. More than warmth. There was pain. Even then, so many years later, I could see it where I knew others couldn't. I didn't want to cause any more pain. I trod lightly.

Despite my stupor, I'd made a calculated decision to fish for more information. Abby was the first person I actually knew here in this whatever world I was in. The doc said she was my wife. Well, he said my wife lived in this house. If I blurted out the truth, or what seemed like the truth, we would only wind up talking about whether it was true.

I needed more. What did wife mean? Past or present? Maybe the hallucination was about her all along. Maybe she could end it. So I did my best Cary Grant and fed her a line about how I'd been thinking about the old days and thought I'd drop over and then I made up some business about being exhausted and how that moment at the door caught me by surprise and I was feeling more like my old self every minute.

Of course, I hadn't felt like my old self for the last two hours, but I was feeling better. That much was true.

She bought it, sort of. I never could lie to her, but since the truth felt like a lie, my lie didn't sound like a lie normally would.

"What old days were you thinking about?" she asked.

Bad opening. I had no information to give. Except for Nebraska, I didn't know any old days and it looked like, for the purposes of my hallucination anyway, there had been 16 years of them. When you have to reach, reach for a cliché.

"When we were just getting started," I said.

"You mean, Nebraska, before we left?"

Okay, I had the first toehold.

"Yeah."

"So, you want me to tell you about us." Abby said it without a trace of sarcasm, but more than a trace of inquiry. "What brought this on?"

"I heard a piece of music." It passed my lips before my brain okayed it. I surprised myself, but realized it was true. There were pieces of music, not songs, just pieces of music, that had returned her to me for 16 years. It was always a pleasant reunion, but it always ended in regret.

Gray Jarvis came to me. Well, he didn't, but another one of his insights, did. "You can't cash in a regret. All your life you make, you build. From nothing, you create something. Where something wasn't, now there's a pile of something. When you get older you can go back into that pile and it will nourish you. Regrets are holes in the pile. Reach in and you'll pull out nothing."

"Alright, I'll tell you about us," she said. "Well, to begin with, you're not at work."

Gray's voice went away and I returned to the couch, from which I still labored to unfold myself. I was not at work. This was correct, as far as it went. It depended on what she meant by work. I needed more.

"Work."

"Matt. It's Monday. Monday at Andrews Advertising and it's after one o'clock."

"I'm supposed to be there."

It sounded like a statement. Actually, it was a question.

"He states the obvious."

She waited. Nothing from me.

"And, I'm supposed to be here because it's your turn to be there because it's your one day to run things all by yourself, even though you don't actually try because you hate having to be there at all," she said. "One day. Even I need a break. And you're supposed to know that. And what on earth is the matter with you? Tell me again. Why did you say 'Help me'?"

"Dizzy. I think it's a virus. The tea is helping. Apologies for the drama."

"You said it was exhaustion."

Caught. I didn't squirm. She dropped it, but I knew she shelved the prevarication somewhere in her brain. She shifted back into her chair. How do women sit on their feet like that? I knew about half of her was persuaded, but I didn't know which half. Time to go deep.

I leaned forward, too, and escaped the clutches of the couch. Unfolded at last, I would start a genuine conversation. I went to the last moment we were together. It was all I had.

"I was thinking. I was thinking about that night. That night in Nebraska. You and I in the street. Your father and brothers on the way."

Everything changed. It was like a glow came over her. I didn't need to push anymore. She fell back and looked upward.

"You were magnificent."

Magnificent. I didn't expect that one. Abby rolled on. Her

60

voice softened. She was in a world of her own. You could tell she loved telling this story.

"When your truck came back around that corner, I knew you were a goner. Then you stood up to Dad and said, 'If you want to kill the father of your grandchild, go ahead.' One after another, my brothers hit you. You never fought back. You just kept getting back up. You just kept saying, 'I love her.'"

I said it. I said that I loved her, still not directly to her, but I said it, at least in this hallucination, on the same night I realized I'd never said it in the real world. Now I needed more.

"Us in Nebraska. You know, before we left," I said. "I want to hear about it in your voice. Pretend I have amnesia."

"It was after school."

School. What school? High school? Maybe she went to college. I tried another dodge. I needed to get her on a roll.

"Oh, yeah, those days."

"After we forced you to finish high school."

We. Who was we? Detective prevarication time.

"Yeah, you really worked me over."

"Well, you'll recall it was Dad more than me. He really ended up caring about you, not that you ever noticed."

She got the dig in. She eyeballed me hard. The concern crept back onto her face. Now she was talking and measuring me at the same time.

"And then the mail-order art school and then the scholarship to MU. God, those were great years. Then it was either here or Chicago. Remember when we flipped the coin?"

Goosebumps. Luckily, she went on.

"We flipped and we flipped and it kept coming up Chicago until we threw it away and voted against the cold and here we came. I've wanted those early days here in California back so many times. You doing commercial work. Me painting."

She cocked her head just so and eyed me up and down.

"What are we doing? What is this memory lane routine? It's not like you weren't there."

I gave her my look that's the equivalent of a shrug. It didn't work. She leaned forward again.

"You haven't used profanity since we started talking."

She didn't try to hide the curiosity.

"Or smoked a cigarette.

Her body shifted in the chair. She was wearing athletic clothes. Athletic clothes. This was new. Abby the gym rat. Her form shifted, and I couldn't avoid watching. I brought out the firehose again. I didn't put it away.

"I saw the famous floorscape painting today at the museum," I said. I wanted to insert a swear word, but it didn't feel natural.

This one braked the train. She gave me a long penetrating look. A very long very penetrating look.

The weather in the room changed to partly cloudy. Make that cloudy. Just like that, her pain had returned and, along with it, my shame, although I wasn't sure why.

"This amnesia thing. You sure it's not real?"

It was spill-the-beans time. I would do it. No, it wasn't. I would wait.

"I just want to hear our story. In your words."

I was just saying words. Anything to pause the pain and shame.

"The painting ruined you, and us."

That was Abby. She never came at anything sideways. She was speaking as though I did have amnesia, explaining me to me.

"Ruined," I said.

"There's no other way to put it. We built your commercial

art shop into a full-fledged advertising studio. It just took off. We had half a floor in a building downtown. Contract artists. Assistants. Bookkeepers. I was working there, too, by that time. Then the painting comes out."

"Comes out."

"It wins Best in Show at the MOCA annual. It's all fine at first. We get the prize money and the party and the showing and the publicity. Really helped our business. That's when the articles start appearing."

"Articles."

"First in some oddball publications, then mainstream papers. Then the Times and then national magazines. Half the people embrace the idea."

"Idea."

Abby grew quiet. She took a pull off her tea cup and uncurled her legs and shifted to the front of the chair again, her eyes searching mine as she spoke.

"What the hell are you doing?"

I gave her my empty look. Again.

"Tell me you don't know this."

I gave her my about-to-shrug look.

"Why do you want to relive this?"

Her face had lost all purchase. It was unreadable.

"Because I'm sitting at a lunch counter in Atlanta."

I had no idea where that came from. Abby tensed. No, it was more than that. Her body became a fist.

"Okay, here we go again."

You could read her face now. It was telling me that the contempt and the pain couldn't be contained.

"So, we're trying on another persona, are we? Don't answer. Oh, for God's sake, Matt."

Well, I hadn't heard that one for sixteen years. Perhaps I should have felt a new shame, but I didn't know what I'd done. Time to grovel.

"No. No! I mean, no. I'm…I'm me. Nothing's new. Well, today's been a little different, but…"

"A diner in Atlanta."

It was a statement and a question and an opening, all at once. With continued contempt.

My turn.

"It was a bad attempt at poetic license. I wanted you to envision a scene. It's like you are sitting next to a person in another place and telling him about the painting."

This saved the moment. Not bad, considering. I watched her body fist unclench, almost all the way.

Still my turn. "Idea," I said.

"Okay," she said. It was an ellipsis okay, as opposed to an exclamation point okay, but it would do. She wasn't sold, but she was still in the store, so to speak. She went on.

"The idea. The idea that the painting reveals an ancient mystery. That the objects in the painting – letters and symbols from the Hebrew alphabet – can be interpreted as a code. That the code can be solved."

I gave her my is-that-it look. When she returned it, I knew that she knew this wasn't a game. She understood I actually had no clear memory of these events. I watched her file this next to my earlier prevarication, and for the first time in this new world I grasped just how deeply we understood each other. She watched me as I watched her decide to continue this sham. And then she knew that I knew, and kept on anyway.

"That the Hebrew letters of the first sentence of Genesis predict the coming of Christ."

I'm sure what she saw in my eyes was a thousand-yard stare. She gently, ever so gently, reached out and put her hand under my chin. It was the first time we'd touched in that way in this otherworldly world. She pushed my chin up and closed my mouth, which notified me that it had been hanging open. She stroked my cheek. It was electric. I had goose bumps I didn't want. Firehose.

She went on. "The other half think the idea is nuts. And maybe you, too. Or, you're just a modern version of Barnum."

"It's just junk on my floor."

I said it through my thousand-yard stare. A huge regret entered the room. Monstrous big. It wanted me to know it was there, just so it could watch. Abby knew it was there, too, only she knew why it was there, and I didn't. I could tell she was tiring of the fiction.

"Well, that was your story at first. The painting came to be known as the 'mirror of the Sistine Ceiling' and well, let's just say you caught yourself in the mirror."

"Ruined," I said.

Her hands moved to my cheeks. She turned my face to hers. She was impossibly gentle. Our eyes met.

"Fame and money, Matt. You didn't wear them well."

Her eyes traveled across my black outfit and back to mine. "You still don't."

She took her hands away. "I thought all we needed was a blue ribbon, some publicity, and some prize money. I should have known you needed more."

Again, the eyes on my clothes. "To say the least, I didn't see this coming."

Abby. Always straight with you. I had a half a picture, but I wanted the rest. I didn't get to hear it.

We both alerted at the sound of the front door closing. It was unmistakable – a thud instead of a click. Then easy footsteps down the hall. A teenaged girl breezed in and tossed her books into a chair, stopping when she saw me.

She lit up. "Dad! You're here!"

Goosebumps again. Instantly, you could tell she was ours, even though she was blonde. She got the best of Abby and the parts of me that didn't hurt her. Yet another push and pull. I was drawn to her, instantly attached in the same way I was joined with Annie in the delivery room.

Annie. Where was Annie? She was mine. This one was mine, too, except in a hallucination. It was torture. My heart, which had slid back where it is supposed to be in those few moments on the couch with Abby, returned to the top of my chest. With it came the tightness and the quick breath and the sense that my skin was on fire. In other words, the way I'd felt since I woke up in this new world.

What is her name? I knew I should know it. I didn't want to ask. I couldn't ask. I wanted to stay, but I had to go. My only relief, such as it was, was moving. Then, even if I didn't know where I was, I could feel like I was going somewhere.

I bolted from the room. It wasn't a choice. My feet and legs did it on their own. I didn't look at their faces. I didn't want to see shock and dismay. I was already filled with too much of both.

✳✳✳

You can't walk home in Los Angeles. You can't walk anywhere in Los Angeles. This had fully dawned on me when Abby pulled up alongside as I walked in the street. I don't know how far

66

I'd walked. I'd spent the time hating myself and the way I left things in that house, but I couldn't turn back. My hallucination daughter, with her outburst of 'You're here!' supplied the one fact I was afraid to ask Abby about.

It also told me I knew I didn't live in the house with them. I stopped walking. Abby's motor idled.

"Get in."

It was an order. I obeyed. I worked on the assumption that I lived somewhere, even in this nightmare, and she knew where that was.

"Can you take me home?"

I think it was the sound of my own voice that did it. It was so small and pitiful. I began to weep. I couldn't hold it back. It's actually a relief when you let anguish go, even if you still want to curb it. I realized I'd spent most of the day holding back a low-beam rage, almost like when I was a kid. But now I knew there was nothing to fight, so the spasms and the tears came. And me, a grown man. Abby touched my arm. Every fiber of my being wanted to reach over and embrace her.

"Please don't," I said. My voice was still tiny. She withdrew. I could tell I'd hurt her. I touched her arm. It was the first time I touched her. It was like touching a high voltage wire. I could feel her passing through me.

"It's not your fault," I said. I knew that she knew I meant it. She faced the windshield and drove.

The day was waning when Abby dropped me at my address. Wherever you are in Los Angeles, it's not near. It was the longest wordless drive I ever took. There in the car, she left me alone as I calmed down and watched the city I had genuinely come to loathe in only one day pass by. When I saw my house, or at least the house Abby pointed out as mine, I loathed it, too.

We stopped. I got out and closed the door. She leaned out through the window.

"You know we still love you," she said. "Always have."

Once, when Gray and I were talking, he used the word "lacuna." When I asked him what it meant, he explained that a lacuna is a place where something should be, but there's nothing there. This is what I'd become. A lacuna. There was no place to put their love.

Luckily, she didn't wait for a reply. I watched her go, and kept watching after she was gone.

My hallucination address was an expensive address. You could see the Pacific. I thought about Atlanta. It would be dark there now. If any of this were real, Jill would wonder, but not worry.

Jill. I hadn't thought of her while I was with Abby. Another reason to dislike myself.

I had hallucination cash. Four thousand dollars and change. I could go to the hallucination airport and be in Atlanta in four hallucination hours. The idea panicked me. It brought to the front of my mind the awful thing that been at the back since I awoke in the museum. What if nobody was there? No Jill, no Annie, no Mitt, no me, no house, no job. A life of lacunas.

I found the key by looking in the first stupid place I would hide one. I went inside. Instantly, I was offended by my own taste.

Another Gray Jarvis observation played out before me in cringe-inducing vividness. "The only thing that never changes is the avant-garde."

It was the kind of self-consciously modern furniture that makes you long for escape. It's awful and as comfortable as it looks, which means you never want to use it. Your brain may consider a chair to be a statement. Your behind doesn't. It was an open, sterile layout. Lots of glass. There were points where curves should be and curves where curves didn't want to be. Flat, loud hues, like color farts.

The angry artist in the museum had called me an asshole. He may have been on to something. My home looked, and felt, like a lounge. A lounge at a motel that had the word "Atomic" in its name. It didn't scream "bachelor pad," it groaned it.

I made the cringe and wince tour. The round bed. The "conversation pit." The overdone bar. The disingenuous art. I opened my closet, a walk-in. Elaborate, like the lighting was from a store. Every article in there was black. I, too, wore the mandatory uniform of non-conformity.

Quick survey of the room. It dawned on me that I had a cleaning service. The real Atlanta me picked up after himself. The hallucination me would never do that. I knew there would be a studio around somewhere. When I found it, I knew the cleaning service hadn't been allowed inside.

Picture my Nebraska house and you're most of the way to seeing my studio, with one big difference. There were no finished canvasses. Some were half-finished. The rest didn't get that far. Each had two things in common. They all tried to replicate the look of the museum painting. They all failed. The room made me tired. I couldn't get out fast enough.

And then, there it was, in a hallway. The telephone, the opposite of a lacuna. It brought the cringe tour to a standstill. It was a thing that had been there all day, posing a very simple question. Was I seconds away from talking to Jill? I picked up the receiver. I put down the receiver. I picked it back up. I turned it in my hand and looked at it. I had no idea what I was looking for. I put it back down. I walked away. I turned around. I walked back. I picked it up again. I put it down again.

I didn't bother to count how many times I did this routine. I just know that eventually I rushed to the phone, picked it up, poked my own phone number into it and held my breath. After about five million rings, a strange voice answered. I hung up as fast as I could. Can you make a mistake in a hallucination? Yes. I just did, which is why I was grateful when I realized it was too late to call work and see if Helen the receptionist knew I existed. I made my gloomy eyes-toward-the-floor way down the hall, and didn't look back at the phone.

I didn't eat anything at the diner. It seemed so long ago. Well, it was long ago, food-wise. I had hallucination hunger, which as near as I could tell was exactly like real hunger. I went to my sterile, hallucination kitchen and popped the fridge. It was a bachelor's fridge. Nothing to cook. A few things to eat. There was beer. Hallucination me still liked beer, so I had one as I bolted some leftover Chinese.

I was in a hurry to sleep, so I could awaken in Atlanta, but the sun was still out. It was setting in the Pacific and making a show of it, but I wasn't in the mood for breathtaking.

I flipped on the television. Monday Night Football. Playoff game. For a moment, I took this as proof of hallucination. It was Monday night, but it was early. Then I factored in the time change and it all shifted into normal. Could I have cared less about the game? No. But the enthusiastic TV mumbling and bleeping felt familiar and so it stayed on. Another beer, which almost made me feel like my old self, until I realized I was living in my older old self and didn't like him.

Sports announcers do three things. They tell you what you are about to see. Then they tell you what you are seeing. Then they tell you what you saw. We were in phase one. I used it as

70

background noise as I pulled a sheet of paper and outlined the day. With the exception of the nurse's bosom, everything had been in scale. The strange part was that all the strangeness was staged in front of an otherwise normal backdrop. No wraiths or snakes or living skulls. It was their absence that made it creepy. The banality made it all cold. I couldn't shake the feeling that it just didn't feel like an illusion.

I pushed the paper away. The beer was kicking in. It was the best I'd felt since the diner. I considered a third.

In the background, I could hear the announcers heading into phase two. The game was about to begin. I looked up, and the screen arrested me. The referee and the team captains were grouped for the coin flip.

Was this slow motion? The camera followed the coin after the ref tossed it and it zoomed in as the coin landed. It was a fifty-cent piece. You could also see that the coin was in black and white while everything around it was in color. Then I watched as a black and white hand entered the screen, reached down and picked up the coin.

Heads.

Everything went black.

IV

DAY TWO

For the second time that day, the electric thump and trill faded. I took my bearings. In the dark and chill, I recognized the oh, so welcome sidewalk outside my house in Atlanta. For a moment, I just stood there, grateful. I noticed I was gripping a bag. I checked the contents. Bottle of wine.

A quick audit – bent pinky, bent nose, familiar non-black clothing, snow. I was home. Home to windows lighting the night. Home that was warm and uplifting.

Everything was normal, except it wasn't. A time check put me on the east coast version of the hour and minute I exited my Los Angeles hallucination. I braced myself for who-knows-what and entered my house.

"Great! You're back."

Jill peeked out of the kitchen and greeted me after the door closed. Apparently, I'd gone somewhere other than Los Angeles. I looked at the wine bottle, and it dawned on me that I needed to launch another detective routine.

Jill sounded perfectly natural. No kids – past their bedtime.

The snow gear pile, which I had left in the hall that morning, told me it was the same day. Jill breezed in, swiped the wine out of my hand and made for the family room.

"Sorry to send you out on a night like this."

I'd been sent out, which meant I'd already been home.

She paused at the entrance to the family room. "You gonna watch this with your coat on?"

This. A movie. Normal.

I discarded the detective act and headed, coatless, for the couch and some motion picture fiction that couldn't hold a candle to my own. I didn't have to ask questions. Jill chatted and painted a picture of my day. I had come home from work as usual. I had played with the kids as usual. Then, there was dinner – spaghetti – a bath for the kids, bedtime reading and Jill noticing we were out of wine and me as errand boy. And now, the couch in the dark and a movie.

As near as I could tell, I had been there when I wasn't there. I lost nine waking hours. Did I sleepwalk through them? It was a nine-hour lacuna. Part of me was dying to fill it. Part of me was afraid to. What if I had done something awful? Did I still have a job? Heaven only knows what I could have said to Haman. Panic came and went like surf. Outwardly, there didn't seem to be anything noteworthy or curious, at least from Jill's perspective. I told myself it was an aberration. Maybe it was food poisoning. I told myself I was strong enough in character to stay in character even in the grip of a mind-erasing condition. I had done nothing wrong. It was an apparition. That was it.

So, why did my mouth taste like Chinese food? And why could I still feel the two beers?

That wasn't the only aftertaste. The shame that had draped over me at Abby's still hung there. It weighed a ton, maybe two. I had spent nine hours as the old me. The old dismal me. I didn't despise him, I pitied him. But others did despise him, and apparently for good reason, which is one of the many reasons why over the years I had rarely turned my thoughts to any event that occurred before Gray dragged me out of my burning truck.

I turned to watch Jill's face. Her profile came and went as the movie flickered. She looked content. She was content. I knew I made her content and happy with me. I had never willfully given her a reason not to be.

Jill was, and always would be, my dance partner. I wanted her. Other than office hours, we were pretty much constant companions. The want was on a toggle switch that was permanently in the on position. It was just a matter of degree. It was like there was a glow around her and I was gauging the intensity minute by minute.

The desire Abby had evoked in me ranged from forceful to ferocious. It may have been an illusion, but it still felt authentic. It felt authentic because traces of it were still there. That night Jill watched a movie I will never recall while I held a firehose on visions of Abby. Illusion or no, I had a benumbed sense that I had two wives. I already knew then I wasn't going to get any sleep.

✳✳✳

They say if you move the same piece of paper on your desk three times, it means you don't know what to do with it. I had just completed move number two. It was a newspaper clipping on my drawing table and, yes, I didn't know what to do with it. There really wasn't anything I could do other than stare.

I was in my office in Atlanta, jittery after a sleepless night.

When you spend the day in a nightmare, you fear real sleep. Now, the morning was no better. I one-eyed the clipping again and failed to put any of this together. Every logic was round. Every fact was square.

A low cough and some shuffling behind me brought me back to the moment. It was Joel from the morgue. The morgue is newspaper lingo for the library of clippings and photos from past editions, all dated, categorized and filed. There is also research material, shelves of it – maps, almanacs, city directories, dictionaries, encyclopedias, books of government data, stuff like that.

Joel, I knew. I saw him daily, usually more than once, mostly for reference photos for caricatures or objects I wanted to draw. He preferred the word "morgue" to the word "library." His avocation was all things inscrutable. It could be supernatural or just plain peculiar, he didn't care. He wanted to know about it.

You could underestimate Joel. People did. His hair looked like he just got out of bed and his clothes looked like he slept in them. That and his thick glasses could combine to paint a deceptive picture. I knew him to be smart, and you could tell he sensed that. For me, Joel delivered. Everybody else trudged to the library to get their own files.

"Do you know that guy?" he said, gesturing toward the twice-touched clipping he'd delivered earlier.

There was a photo and a headline and a news story. In the photo, the angry artist from my Los Angeles hallucination stood before a too familiar large black square. He wasn't angry in the photo. He was studiously casual, his face tightened into that penetrating gaze inconsequential people and fashion models use when they want to look like they discovered the breakthrough for all that matters. The headline read "Twenty-three, Sixty-nine,

76

Five Added to Museum Collection."

The story identified him as Jeremiah Mora.

"Yes and no," I said. I didn't look up from the clipping. Joel didn't pursue the question further.

He shuffled again and coughed again. I turned to him.

"Apologies, Joel. I guess I'm...I'm distracted."

"He's after you."

How did Joel know? Did our scene at the museum make the hallucination news? You could tell Joel saw a question in my eyes. He clarified.

"E. Farley Haman."

Okay, that I knew. I gave Joel my keep-it-coming look.

"Everybody knows he hates you."

"Joel, any fool can start a quarrel."

"He sent for files on you. All of them. Your family. Where you lived. Where you went to school, especially school."

Another keep-it-coming look.

"You and me, us, we're the only people on the top floors who didn't go to college. Farley makes sure I know that."

"Joel, everybody needs somebody to look down on." I could tell Joel wanted some context. "Farley saw my resume. I didn't keep any schools a secret. There weren't any. Let him sweat it."

"He wants dirt on you."

"Never trust a man who parts his name on the side."

"He keeps asking. He says you were a delinquent."

"Guilty."

"He says he knows you have something to hide."

"I don't."

The words came out without a thought, but thoughts followed. I may or may not have fathered a child out of wedlock. Nobody knew this. Not Gray. Not even Jill. I never considered it a secret.

It was just an invisible something from a previous life I wanted to put away. That I had put away. Buried.

Then the events of the previous day washed over me. It wasn't a warm bath. For the first time in a long time, I began to realize there were some things I could never put away.

I heard shuffling. I returned to the moment and saw Joel watching me, uneasy. He produced another file.

"Here's the other one you wanted."

I took the file and pulled a solo clipping. It was a brief bio of the emergency room doctor who treated me in hallucinogenic Los Angeles. I placed it on the drawing table, pretty sure I'd move it at least two more times.

They were real, the artist and the doc, and they were there in Los Angeles. And Twenty-three, Sixty-nine, Five was one very real and very large and very lame piece of modernism.

The clippings were unsettling but, somehow, not surprising, like the aftertaste of beer and Chinese. I push-pinned the clippings to my corkboard. At least I would stop moving them around. Deadline approached.

Joel again. "And here's the book."

He handed me The Hebrew Aleph-Beyt: History and Interpretation. It was a thumb-worn old book, and I gave Joel my attaboy look.

"Only you would have this on hand."

Joel was more than ready to continue. Not many people shared his interests and here I was nosing in one of them.

"The letters in the Hebrew alphabet are also numbers. Like in Greek, except the letter forms are based on precise symbols and it's real complicated."

He shuffled again.

"I couldn't find Abigail Alexander, not in California or that town in Nebraska. She isn't well-known. There's no profile."

I gave him my that's-okay look.

"No ad agency. No artist's portfolio. No police record. She's never been in the news."

"No sweat, Joel. It was a long shot."

He looked relieved as he went on his way.

✳✳✳

Drawing isn't thinking. Thinking is thinking. You'd be surprised how many people who consider themselves artists can't grasp this. It's especially true of political cartoonists. It is why most political cartoons are forgettable.

People ask cartoonists where the ideas come from. There is an answer, at least for me. Ideas are like wild animals, hiding in plain sight everywhere. You have to see one, catch it and wrestle it to the ground. Then you stroke it until it purrs and let it go. If you have a daily deadline like mine, you see dozens of ideas. You catch some, wrestle a few of them to the ground, and stroke a few of them, but only one will purr.

That's the one you let go.

There are a few standard schools of lousy editorial cartoon ideas. If you come across a 'toon employing any of these, you can be sure the cartoonist doesn't understand thinking.

The first is the Roller Coaster School, a magnificent illustration of things that go up and down. Stock markets. Political careers. Weather. The list goes on.

The second is the Maze School. This haunting exercise in draftsmanship just sings out how complicated a thing can be.

This school is great for any issue involving choice, which is any issue. This list is longer.

The third school is the Sinking Ship, which has two working themes. One theme works best if the cartoonist cleverly insinuates that the occupants of the ship aren't aware it is sinking. The other theme illustrates occupants fully aware of the trouble, which itself has two sub-themes: the desperately bailing theme and the wry acceptance theme. This list is shorter.

When I looked down to see my hand penciling a man in a sinking boat, I knew the drawing zone was closed for the day.

Actually, I was able to get in the zone, but I couldn't stay in it. I couldn't close the trapdoor in my brain. Yet another mind-twister from the day before would nose it open before the door snapped down. There were so many twisters, but one wouldn't go away. The colorless fifty-cent piece.

Okay, coins are black-white, but they're not. They are shades of silver and they reflect color. The hand and the sleeve had no color. Okay, that could be the lighting, but the lighting in a diner and a football stadium isn't the same.

And I was physically in the diner. I wasn't black and white.

You can't think or draw when your own brain is nagging you like one of those tiny itches that won't let you sleep. When the trapdoor wants to open and you push it down, but the door resists and there's a gap and there's white noise from the other side and it gets louder as the gap widens, you can't think.

I pushed the chair away from the drawing table and pulled a 'toon out of my sick day file. Every cartoonist with a daily deadline has one – a cache of workmanlike pieces or ideas on evergreen topics. Done, ready to go, or almost done, ready in minutes. This one was ready to go. Sometimes you gotta phone it in. I called in a copyboy and called it a day. It wasn't noon.

***

What is normal doesn't have to be absolutely normal. For me, a normal workday began with me acknowledging that Hawaii is pronounced with a "v" sound and then enduring the Haman gauntlet before coffee cup number three. I promise if you try it, day in and day out, it will begin to feel normal, but you'll know it isn't. It's like every day is a sentence that starts with a stutter.

Normally, I would abbreviate the morning stutter. It's an efficiency thing. I was always pleasant with Helen, but kept it brief, and I was generally uncivil with poor old Farley. Today had been different. I lingered with Helen, silently probing for any hint that yesterday afternoon wasn't normal. You could tell she was surprised someone, anyone, actually paused and listened. Two minutes with her told me that I had, indeed, returned from the diner and that I had been my same old self and that the coffee in Havaii is more flavorful than diner coffee. Much more flavorful.

I tried to pause a bit and be civil with Farley, but it was no use. My behavior was way out of context for him and he didn't know what to do with it. I didn't close my door on him. He closed his door on me. So, I went with the Helen report and left it at that. I had been where I was supposed to be, and I had been in another world in my mind at the same time. Somehow, it was a relief to know I was in two places at one time. Or whatever.

The copyboy snagged the 'toon. Time to go. Hall. Elevator. Lobby. With a backward wave to Helen, I hit the sidewalks of Atlanta and made for the diner. The scene of the crime. It seemed like the only logical place to go, if logic could be applied at all, and I got there fast.

It's tricky to discern abnormal in a diner. Everything, everybody, fits in. Still, that was my self-assigned task. To case the joint after the fact. I needed clues, and my idea was to re-enact the previous day. I was early, so it was easy to take the same seat at the counter I'd used the day before. Same waitress. Same smile. A Number Five? I didn't smile back. I searched her face. Had she seen anything extraordinary yesterday, perhaps something like, say, me vanishing? I searched too long. She lowered her pad and pencil and eyed me. I returned to the moment and delivered the usual return smile. Yes, a Number Five. She called me honey and swept away.

I searched the room. The grill man conducted a lilting Tchaikovsky for the waitress ballet. So little space. So much grace. How do they keep air between each other? When I tried to be stealthy, I felt stupid. The coffee came. Another eye search. The customers were being customers. Nobody acknowledged me. The space atop my stool was a lacuna, and I was in it.

I reached into my pocket and pulled out The Letter. Another eye search. Nothing. It was still the lull before the noon rush. I scanned the letter for the thousandth time.

I vaulted from my stool like there were springs under it, threw some money on the counter like they do in the movies and almost bent the door on my way out. I hit the sidewalk running. Later that day, it dawned on me that the waitress actually did see me vanish this time.

No time for musings. The most important meeting of my professional life was in five minutes and I had forgotten it. I had a lunch date with the syndicate brass, and if I hadn't pulled out The Letter, I would have missed it.

Time for self-castigation. How could I have forgotten this? Time for self-consolation. I was, after all, still in recovery from a day-long mind trip. I calculated that I could make it to the meeting without a sweat-inducing sprint. The half-speed lope that people use at airports would get me there on time.

I took stock of myself as I slalomed slow-motion pedestrians and the occasional orphan pile of snow. I was grateful that I'd taken care to go through every step of my morning routine before I left the house, which meant I sported the standard shower and shave under a standard jacket and tie. I didn't look like an oil painting, but I looked okay.

My run hop arrested mid-hop, and I just stood there, idling somewhere between anguish and annoyance. Tomorrow's cartoon was an evergreen. It was mediocre, because all evergreens are mediocre. The syndicate boys would see it. It wasn't a deal killer, but it wasn't a deal sealer, either. Sometimes, the only thing you can do is shrug. I decided to just hate myself and started loping again.

I got there dead on time.

The meeting was scheduled for a restaurant that occupied the penthouse floor of a circular tower that dominated the Atlanta skyline like an overlarge silo. The joint had a gimmick. It was a slow-motion revolving restaurant, and if you sat there for an hour and a half or so, you'd make the full circle and get the full view of the South's Most Ambitious City. If you went there for a lunch meeting, after the handshaking and napkin rustling, you knew the first few minutes of conversation would be about the novelty. And so it was.

We were four, with me near the window on my side of the table. Across from me sat the syndicate's editorial director and sales director. Next to me was Hank, whose title escaped me. I still have no idea why he was there, but if I had to guess, it was because he was superb company at cocktail hour on an expense account road trip.

The restaurant was a cloth napkin room with ballpark pricing. You paid for the view, which cost a dollar per adjective. If "peas" were a buck in any other restaurant, "farm fresh peas" were three bucks here. The syndicate boys didn't care. Expense account lunch. When the first round of drinks arrived, I had a flash from the doctor in my hallucination emergency room. Drinking at noon again.

We labored through the menu and sent the waiter on his way. We small-talked through two courses, mostly beauty-parlor stuff about the industry. Hank was a talker. You could tell he knew the industry and everyone in it. You could tell because the other two listened. When they stopped listening, it was down to business. The sales director explained the benefits of syndication like maybe every cartoonist in the country didn't know them by heart – fame and money, money and fame. They would sell and distribute my cartoons to newspapers across the country. There was potential for a huge audience. I didn't interrupt. He liked saying it and I liked hearing it.

He moved from there into the benefits of his particular syndicate. For this, I leaned forward. It dawned on me that they had a contract ready in one of those briefcases. I pictured myself slapping my forehead. Well, of course they did. Why come here? A contract. I didn't see much point in being coy. They may or may not have known that I had no other offers and that tomorrow's 'toon was an evergreen and that I would sign pretty much anything they put in front of me.

That's when I realized I hadn't told Jill about this. Another victim of yesterday.

The sales director's voice brought me back around. It had that I'm-wrapping-it-up sound. "So, that's our pitch. We think you and Universal are a natural fit. And we think you are ready for the big stage."

The editorial director leaned in. "We understand the audience that understands you. You know, we're headquartered in Kansas City. Flyover country. Family values."

That's when Hank produced a fifty-cent piece. A fifty-cent piece.

He was ever so casual. I wasn't. He began to manipulate the coin. It appeared and disappeared in his palm. The others two took no notice. Hank hardly noticed it himself. It was just something he did.

Well, I noticed. Before yesterday, I hadn't seen a fifty-cent piece in years. Now, here was a third one showing up while the first two still made me nervous. I couldn't take my eyes off it. I realized my mouth was hanging open. I could feel my pulse accelerate. I tried to break the spell.

"So, how does this proceed?" I said. Hank began to do a knuckle roll with the coin. It tumbled across his fingers, pinky to index, and into his palm and then back up his pinky.

"We aren't going to bundle you," the sales director said.

"Bundle." I repeated the word like I was hypnotized, which I was, sort of.

Rivulets of sweat percolated and trickled beneath my shirt. What if he dropped the coin? What if he flipped it? The events of the day before began knocking on another door in my brain.

Why was I picturing Abby?

The sales director's voice again. "Package you with other cartoonists in one sale. We're not doing that. You'll be a one-off sale. Sort of an exotic, in a backward kind of way."

"Exotic." I repeated it like a zombie, now thoroughly entranced.

I tried to discern color in the coin. Was it silver or just black and white? The knock on my brain door became a push, and the door started to give way. Fingers and hands. A lacuna on the other side. Static. I heard a girl I'd never met say "Dad." I pushed back. Somewhere between the door in my brain and the coin in Hank's hand, there was a conversation going on around the table before me that I needed to pay close attention to, but I wasn't.

The editorial director leaned in again and broke the moment. "Your voice is distinct, but has broad appeal at the same time. Look, 90 percent of political cartoonists today are saying the same thing. And they say it every day."

Hank fumbled the coin. I startled, which startled my tablemates until I camouflaged the moment by pretending to stop a sneeze, which almost broke my spell. Hank didn't drop the coin. The sales director continued. "You appeal to people with middle-class values. Family. Work. Responsibility. You know, God and country."

The editorial director leaned in. "And we like your drawing style. It's better."

Hank palmed the coin. It didn't reappear. He bent his index finger while his thumb pushed the coin up and balanced it there. He lowered his thumb. He was going to flip it. The door in my brain was easing open. I couldn't stop it, not even with a mental shoulder.

"A lot better," said the sales director. "It's bold, like...like..."

"Modigliani," I said. It came out of nowhere, except it didn't. I could see Abby's mantel and the portrait above it. Instantly I knew I had to get back into the table conversation. I'd tossed them a curve. Outside and high. Modigliani. No art history students at this table. Not a good idea to make people feel uncultured. Hank looked up. He stopped with the coin.

"But, hey, Modigliani was doing Botticelli," I said and gave them the old wry chuckle. They returned it. They knew Botticelli. At least they knew the name. They could still feel sophisticated. Slow fastball in the groove.

Hank flipped the coin toward his other hand. I choked on my own breath. He dropped it and bent over to retrieve it. I still wonder how big my eyes were at that moment.

"Okay boys," Hank's voice came from below the table. "Heads or tails?"

The other two ignored the request. I couldn't speak.

"It was heads," he said.

Heads. East. Here. In my hallucination, heads had sent me home. It felt comical to be relieved, but reassuring nonetheless. The crowd at the door in my brain faded away.

"Your paper here will love it," said Hank. "Your cartoon puts them in every paper in the country. Matt Andrews, the Atlanta Journal. Sign it big."

"And for heaven's sake, make your signature readable," said the sales director. "What is it with cartoonists and their stupid signatures? Don't they understand your name is your most important asset?"

I shifted in my seat. My name. That would be the name that E. Farley Haman was single-mindedly working to discredit. The brain crowd returned for a moment, then faded.

"Speaking of signatures, your next question needs to be

'where do I sign?'" Said Hank.

I gave them my please repeat that look. The editorial director produced a briefcase and shuffled through it.

"We'll need a bio on you for the sales kit," said the sales director. "No arrests for cattle rustling, I assume."

"Today seems to be a personal history day for me," I said.

The head of sales slid the contract toward me. "Take it home. Read it.

The editorial director leaned in. "Get a lawyer. We don't want to be sitting here a year from now with a confused relationship."

Hank pushed a return envelope, addressed and stamped, across the table. You could tell he was done with me and ready for an expense account away game. And then we were standing. We shook hands and tried to think of something to say as the glass elevator lowered us to the street. They went their way. I went mine. It was over. I never touched my drink. I couldn't tell you what I ate.

I was probably a few blocks from the restaurant when I realized I was running. Not airport loping, running. I say probably a few blocks because I had no idea where I was even though I was familiar with the city. People. Noises. Flashes of color. There was a show going on in my brain. A roman candle of impulses. A showcase of fears.

I knew why I was running. It was the only response that made sense. Part of me, much too big a part of me, had wanted Hank's coin to come up tails. I wanted to go back into my hallucination, to see the people on the other side of the door. I wanted to see Abby and this person who was my daughter.

Hold it. Wait, no. I didn't want to go back. I wanted those hands behind the door in my brain to leave me alone. I wanted to go home to Jill and Mitt and Annie.

The pull was gravitational and equally hard to resist. I didn't want to go back, but I did. I didn't. I did. I didn't. I did.

I stopped running on the last "I did." Breathing there, bent. Hands on my knees, eyes bored into the sidewalk. It was a fact. I did want to be in that very real unreality again, and I knew it.

What I didn't know was what it meant. No, I didn't know what it could mean. It was all unknown.

Except, I knew I didn't want to be unfaithful to Jill and Mitt and Annie. I didn't want another life. I didn't want another wife.

That wasn't it. I removed my jacket. I was sweating through it. In January. In snow. I rolled my shirtsleeves past my wrists. Deep breath. I could feel my pulse settle.

What did I want? To know. I wanted to know. I wanted to know about Abby and my otherworldly daughter. I wanted to know about this other me. Who was this dismal person, and why did he feel so real?

Because it *was* real. It was real. It was not possible to simply imagine what I went through. The sights, the sounds, the touches, Twenty-three, Sixty-nine, Five, the painting, the doctor, the bosom, Abby, Modigliani, "Dad," the beer and Chinese. You'd think this would frighten me. It didn't. I felt like I'd just thrown off an anvil. It was real and I'd always known it. It was just a matter of admitting it. That it was also thoroughly impossible didn't seem to matter.

When my breathing returned to normal, I stood erect and took stock of the surrounding facades and storefronts and signs. At least I had run in the right direction. I was a few blocks from the newspaper.

The sights clicked in. Sounds clarified in my ears. Traffic pulse and rhythm and then a little agitation and clamor to my right.

There was a small crowd there, facing the curb, their backs to me. And then I heard above the traffic the unmistakable cadence and tones of a street hustler. A raw, smoke and whiskey voice. I couldn't place it, but it made me queasy even as it pulled me to the fringe of the crowd, behind the rubberneckers and tiptoers.

Why does a bug go toward a flame? Because it wants to. I pushed through until I was front and center. It was three-card monte – hearts – and the guy was an artist, not too fast, not too slow. The patter flowed. My eyes never left the cards. They appeared and reappeared, lifted and dropped, shuffled and dragged, bent just so. And each time he turned over a card, the collective heads of the crowd knocked back in astonishment. He choked out a whiskey-voice chuckle when we gasped. I was hypnotized for the second time that day.

And then I could tell it was my turn. Nobody spoke, I just became aware of it. It was like the hustler and the crowd both picked me. I don't know why. I never took my eyes off the cards. They never stopped moving. Now, the whiskey voice spoke directly to me.

"What, no wager?"

I didn't respond.

"Here, I'll help."

A fifty-cent coin began to appear and disappear and reappear beneath the red and white cards.

They say when you are in the depths of a dream your body is fully paralyzed. I can tell you that when you are in the depths of a dream and you are still awake, your body is fully paralyzed and the radio knob on your hearing turns. It shifts to static. Rushing sound. Voices. Low volume. Speaking too fast. Saying nothing.

And your vision is fixed like you are looking through a tube.

When my vision tube moved upward, I noticed the hustler's hands and wrists for the first time. They were shades of black and white above the red and white cards. And then there were two coins beneath the cards. Fifty-cent pieces. One heads. One tails. They appeared and disappeared and reappeared as the cards were lifted. Heads. Tails. Heads. Tails. Heads. Tails.

Tails.

The hands stopped. The cards went away. One coin remained. Tails. I heard the hustler's raw chuckle. His finger rested on the coin.

It was colorless. Everything went black.

V
TAILS

L ook. Goosebumps!"

The voice was unfamiliar, but I'd heard it before, if that makes sense. I felt the electric moment passing. The blackness faded. Things cleared. Someone's hand held my overdressed black fabric arm, from which extended an unbroken pinky. And a cigarette.

"It must have been something I said," murmured another voice.

This one I knew. Abby. We were outdoors. It wasn't her hand in mine, and it wasn't really a murmur. It was a question that wasn't a question. We walked toward the entrance to a building. My hallucination daughter was on my arm. She'd noticed the goosebumps.

Quick reconnoiter. Sunny day. Pleasant. It was about three o'clock Atlanta time when everything went black. This felt like the California equivalent.

Detective mode. The three of us seemed to be on a mission. You could feel it. Hallucination daughter released my arm. She was also holding Abby's hand. Here we go. I'd have to figure it out.

"I guess I'm just excited," I said. Lame. We – Abby, the daughter whose name I didn't know, and me – stopped. Well, Abby stopped and then we stopped. She was loaded down. Big canvas shoulder bag with an oversized and overstuffed ring binder and one of those big black flat portfolio carrying cases.

"There it is again," Abby said, once more in the question that wasn't a question voice. But there was something else. Many something else's. Wariness. Curiosity. And I knew that penetrating look. Time to stall.

"What is where again?"

I ground the cigarette and dropped it in a trash can.

"Your voice. You don't sound like a jerk. And you aren't littering."

Okay, let's recap. My hallucination wife is comfortable calling me a jerk in the presence of my hallucination daughter. A glance daughter way told me this was not new.

No surprise there – Abby didn't parse words. That my dismal West Coast other-side-of-the-coin self could have the voice of a jerk also didn't come as a surprise. He, I, was a jerk. I guess we all just knew it. I gave Abby my what-gives look.

"The sneer is gone," she said. Another look from me. "From your voice. The sneer is gone. You're like a real person all of a sudden. Ninety-eight point six."

I would have given her my do-you-really-want-to-talk-about-this-now look, but I already knew no topic was off-limits in front of our hallucination daughter, who was now eyeing me, too, just with less wariness and more curiosity. I reached for the canvas bag.

"Let me carry some of this stuff," I said. I knew Abby didn't believe in ghosts. I also knew she just looked like she'd seen one.

94

Apparently, the West Coast me didn't do bags, so I doubled. I took the bag and the portfolio case.

"You were like this yesterday," she said.

Yesterday. That would be hallucinatorily correct, but this moment was too soon. A minute ago, I was underdressed and sweating in an Atlanta winter. Now, my this-side-of-the-coin goosebumps were still fading. I had no clue where we were or why.

I couldn't go on the witness stand. I couldn't even find it. I pled the Fifth with my eyes. Abby moved in front me. It felt like a confrontation, because it was.

"Do you or don't you hate what we're about to do?"

I tried not to look her in the eyes. She touched my chin. High voltage wires again. She moved my face toward hers and lowered my chin. It was either look her in the eyes or close mine. I didn't want to get caught in a lie, which was what her eyes were looking for. Then again, I didn't know what we were about to do. I went with the odds. There aren't that many things I truly hate to do, and I figured we probably weren't going to an opera in the morning.

"No. I don't hate this."

I looked her in the eyes. Now lying wasn't the problem. It was time for the firehose. Her hand slid down my neck and drifted away. She stepped backward. No, she faded backward. Then she came back toward me and got close, searching my face like she was following a treasure map. She stepped away again. Her hands went to her hips. Confrontation again.

"All three of us are going into Andrews Advertising."

She pointed to the entrance. Raised, brushed steel sans-serif too-clean of a font above the door confirmed the name. She wasn't through with the travelogue.

"Together. At the same time. Me. You. Jennifer. And it's okay with you."

Jennifer. My hallucination daughter is named Jennifer. Quick trace. Not a family name. I was glad to know her name.

Was I glad to be here, back in the unreal reality that I had convinced my Atlanta self was real? I had told my Atlanta self I wanted to be here, that I wanted to find out about my hallucination daughter and the dismal me. Well, so far I'd discovered her name and I'd been told I had the voice of a jerk.

Last time all I could think about was going back home. All I wanted was to escape whatever this was. This time I thought I knew I could go back, although I didn't know how. It just felt like I would go back. The last time felt permanent and it smothered me. This time was like a visit. I decided to make the best of it. I still wanted to know more about the dismal me and about the extraordinary painting I knew I didn't paint. Who says you can't enjoy a vacation from reality?

Abby's eyebrows raised one at a time. Right, left, right, left. Time to stop ruminating. I had a question to answer.

Detective mode. Why wouldn't the three of us want to go to work at the same time? Easy, because I was a jerk. Or was it really just two of us who didn't want to go — Abby and I — and Jennifer was a swing player? This seemed to make sense. Jennifer had been holding my arm and Abby's hand. I went corporate style with the answer.

"It just doesn't seem, you know, efficient for both of us to not be there."

Efficient. Best I could do under the circumstances. Both of Abby's eyebrows went skyward.

"Efficient?" She high-pitched this one and delivered another.

"Efficient."

Mock curiosity this time. Now a lower pitch. "Efficient."

She looked at me like I was nuts, which, also under the circumstances, made sense.

"Matt, we have to be here. You and me. At the same time. It's a requirement. The second Tuesday of the month. The Tuesday Lunch. And you hate it."

She said it like it was supposed to be obvious to me, which, of course, it wasn't. All I knew was that I was right about the two-way match. I went with the universal last-ditch reply. I shrugged. It wasn't the right reply. Quick read of Abby. This was too important for a shrug. I added my you're-the-boss look.

"So, you are not going to compete with me in there," she said, again pointing to the entrance.

"Compete," I said. I gave her my you-lost-me look.

Eyebrows skyward again. Her hands fell to her side. If her face was a boiler gauge, the arrow would be wagging in the red.

Jennifer's head was like a swingarm lamp. It went from Abby to me to Abby to me. Whatever this was, she was new to it. Or maybe she knew it and this was the first time she'd seen it out loud.

At second thought, it didn't take much to picture the dismal me as small and petty and jealous of talent. The wardrobe alone screamed it. And something told me that the word "efficient" had never passed the lips of the dismal me. After all, he was the me who never left town that night in Nebraska. The me who never wrecked his truck. The me who was never rescued by Gray Jarvis. He was the me who they said was growing up too fast and then said he didn't grow up at all.

And this, this moment, didn't need to grow. So far it was a two-way match. I didn't want Jennifer dragged onto a tag team. And I didn't want to witness boiler steam.

This, the whole moment, wanted to be very simple.

"No," I said. "I won't compete with you."

I could tell that she could tell I meant it. I breathed. Abby would relax now. She didn't.

"Is this deliberate? This voice. Are you acting or something? What?"

Time to get off the witness stand. I used the only tone I could produce, the one I used when I told my little daughter Annie that no meant no.

"Abby. It's my voice. It's the only voice I have. I don't know why it sounds strange to you. Let's go."

I didn't hate the idea of entering Andrews Advertising, but I didn't relish it, either. I was sure my detective antennae would be at full length for the next I-didn't-know-how-many hours. It would be work.

I headed toward the entrance. Jennifer slipped her arm back into mine. It felt familiar in an impossible way. I looked her way. She had a sunrise smile. You could tell every time she smiled the sun came up anew, with dimples.

Abby trailed us. I felt her eyes on the back of my head.

The place didn't require a second glance. It sang out "ad agency" in full choral forte. Big central room. Airy. Unbarred. Glass offices surrounding the room. You could see through them — all but one — to the streetscape outside. Shiny glass, shiny steel, shiny furniture, shiny appointments. Oversized posters from past campaigns. Awards and trophies. Big plants. Little plants. Warm and cool lighting. Shiny.

But for Abby, the joint would be sterile. Just when you thought everything was a little too bacteria free, there would be something off-kilter, something very Abby, something that punctured the self-conscious hip. You didn't notice them at first

– photos, statuary, gewgaws and gimcracks – but they emerged like details in a photo coming into focus. Then you saw more. The middle of the floor was painted in primary color rectangles and black outlines, like a Mondrian. Actually, it was a Mondrian. Okay, a copy. There were posters on the ceiling.

In the middle of the big room and in the middle of a rigid Mondrian color block was a conference table. All but three chairs were filled. Maybe a dozen faces turned our way. They had "staff" written all over them. They also had a look I'd seen before at the dentist's office. People awaiting root canals. The staff had been watching us through the glass entrance. I didn't speak. I smiled. Abby smiled. Jennifer smiled.

Now it was time for the staff to do the swingarm lamp head move. Abby to me to Abby to me. No detective work here. It was easy to connect these dots. The dismal me ruins moments. Abby saves them. The ball in the air at any moment hardly mattered – an idea, a design, a favorite color – the list probably went to the moon and back.

The staff. It was like they dressed themselves to go with the décor, but they lacked Abby's comic touch. They had rationed themselves in equal measure an aching absence of freshness. No, a weary presence of forced freshness. The black clothes thing – one hundred percent buy-in on that one. Underneath there must be something, and I'm not talking about lingerie. Abby wouldn't hire an empty outfit. And I knew without asking that she did the hiring.

We took our seats. Abby sat at one end of the table. I put the canvas bag and portfolio beside her and went to the other end. Jennifer's chair was in the middle.

Swingarm heads again, only with a wider range.

Lunch. Like I said, I don't do it, even though I had just done it. I've never known how you are supposed to pace it. Chew. Think. Talk. Chew. Think. Talk. There was a forced merriment to it.

If there ever was such a thing as an ad agency lunch box, each staffer had one and no two were the same and they all looked alike. They opened in unison. Napkins. Containers. Bags. Each a little spread.

Once the first bite was down, the chewing swingarms swayed to Abby. All but one. Middle table left. Young and cute and affected. Black pageboy. Black lipstick. Black nails. Black eyeliner and plenty of it. I knew this because the surrounded eyes were unbolted and pleading to me. She wanted a comeback, like maybe I didn't see her. There was a story here and I was sure I didn't want to know it. I gave her my we're-all-here look.

Abby had already opened up the binder and flipped some pages and launched the meeting. No preamble. No chewing. That was Abby. Warm without the fuzzy. She couldn't pretend she cared about how your cat was doing or where you got your chicken salad. Wasn't in her.

I didn't pay attention. This meeting didn't matter to me. Neither did the lunch Jennifer slid over to me. How could it? I'd already had one I couldn't recall. This was just something I had to get through while I examined the unreality of Abby and Jennifer. I watched them both as Abby went through her notes and pulled this and that from her portfolio case.

My first assessment on this side of the coin had been correct. Jennifer looked like us, with extra Abby thrown in. She was engaged in the meeting. She was learning and didn't know it. She watched Abby. Everybody watched Abby. I sensed the staff balked at looking my way. Fear? Intimidation? No. They just preferred to look the other way, except for Black Lipstick Girl. Or maybe there was no point in looking my way.

And Jennifer. I felt that push and pull again. Jennifer drew me in just by being there. I pushed away. I had to.

Abby was cool and professional, warm and approachable. The staff adored her and made no secret of it. Her sunflower voice was like the soundtrack of a training video on management skills. In little time, I became lost in her face and voice. Firehose.

I had hardly cooled down when I noticed every head had swingarmed, mid-chew, my way. Abby was regarding me, too. Had they seen it? Had they sensed the firehose? No. Abby was holding a concept draft from her portfolio case. Apparently, she'd just asked me a question. Time to stall.

"Sorry," I said. "I missed that. Busy admiring the concept sketch."

I knew you could hear a pin drop, because one did. Actually, it was a sandwich. I was in a sea of saucer-sized eyes. I guessed the dismal me didn't admire other people's work very often. And this had to be someone else's work. Neither the real me nor the dismal me could have produced it.

"That's it?" said Abby. "You're good with this?"

My move. I decided to play along.

"What's the client again?"

Abby's tongue pushed her cheek outward. That was her I'm-being-patient look.

"Hotel furniture. Trade show."

That was it. She wasn't giving me more. The swingarm lamp heads came back to me, eyes still saucered, cheeks still chipmunked. My move.

I had given the thing one look. Now, I gave it two.

"Nice logo," I said. Another sandwich dropped, or maybe a pickle. I didn't look.

"You could make it bigger."

The lamp heads swung back to Abby. All but one. Black Lipstick Girl again. Eyes on me. Pleading. Time to escape. Being the freak at the show grows old fast. Also, I wanted to let the staff swallow.

"I need coffee," I said. This was true. I started to push my chair back. So did Black Lipstick Girl.

"I'll get it," I said, "Where's the pot?" Another non-pin dropped. Black Lipstick Girl deflated.

Detective mode. I should know where the pot was. Then again, dismal me probably didn't know where the pot was. Was there a pot? Of course there's a pot. There's always a pot. I looked at Black Lipstick Girl. She pointed toward a door as she slumped back down. Saucer eyes all around. A swallow or two. I made my way there.

Standard issue office kitchen, with the addition of high-grade wiseacre images and slogans and cartoons taped up here and there. I could reach the coffee-maker from the door, so I stood halfway in the frame, which more or less kept me in the big room which allowed Abby to move on, although whatever she was passing on to the staff wasn't for my ears anyway. I was a huge non-factor factor in this building.

And a jerk.

When you see your own name printed somewhere, it catches your eye. My name caught mine. It was on a clipping taped to the cabinet door above the coffee pot. A page from a slick magazine. My name was a kicker headline. Above it was a photo of me standing before the celebrated floorscape painting, decked in all black and doing a "who-me?" shrug.

Below my name was the main headline.

"Bunco Boy or Touched by an Angel?"

So, even hallucination me is two different people.

Byline: Donna Robin Glaser. All three names. I read on:

> *One thing you can say about one-hit-wonder Matt Andrews – he always sticks to the script. Interviewed last week at his dustbin of an office at Andrews Advertising in Los Angeles, he steadfastly avows the absence of a motif for Floor, 1967, his masterwork.*
>
> *"It's just junk on my floor," he says, which is what he has always said.*
>
> *His refusal to affirm any intentional central theme has divided theologians everywhere. It's a sharp divide with no grays in the palette, so to speak.*
>
> *If his claim is genuine – that the content of his "floorscape" is unsystematic, that it organized itself as all piles of litter do, at random – then his hand was surely guided by a divine force.*
>
> *If his claim is deceptive – that he deliberately, not to mention artfully, embedded a biblical code onto the canvas – then he has the hand of a charlatan, albeit an ardent, charming, and talented one.*
>
> *Art critics, on the other hand, are less divided. The art world is never of one opinion. Even Mona Lisa has her detractors, but naysayers of "Floor, 1967," or as the wags refer to it – "The Sistine Chapel Floor" – are almost as hard to find.*
>
> *"Andrews took the age-old genre of still life and turned it on its head," says Archibald Albert, acquisitions director at the Los Angeles County Museum of Art, where Floor, 1967, now hangs. "The subject matter is singular. The composition is at once coherent and arbitrary. Even so, his*

inclusion of a moral, or message, concatenates to the genre's Dutch Renaissance lineage."

For what it's worth, this writer found Andrews' claim to be authentic. He wasn't coy or elusive about the painting's motif or lack of it. Also, according to people who know Andrews, his claim that he has never darkened the door of a church, much less opened a Bible, rings true. I could only ask acquaintances. Apparently, he has no friends.

At the same time, Andrews was elusive, as he always has been, about the artistic impulse that launched his masterpiece and his then groundbreaking and now much-imitated brushwork.

One artist, though, seems unwilling to copy Matt Andrews' brushwork – and that's Matt Andrews. The world still awaits his next canvas. Not since he came out of nowhere to win the..."

I stopped reading. Abby had already told me the rest. The article was undated, but the paper was curling and the tape was yellowed. I pushed on the tape to reconnect it. I don't know why. *Concatenates.* Where's E. Farley Haman when you need him?

To the kitchen door. Back to the meeting I wasn't attending.

I leaned on the door frame. The staff swingarmed at my reappearance. I nodded and tipped my coffee to the table to demonstrate I was tuned in, and then I tuned out again. Time for a second look at this agency. This was the business we built.

We. I use the term loosely. Except for the one room with the covered windows, which was no doubt glutted with my signature rubbish, there was nothing of me – by this, I mean West Coast hallucination jerk me – in this agency. It was all done by Abby.

104

You could tell and I didn't need to be told.

It overwhelmed me with pity. What she did. How she managed. What it took to make this happen while hallucination me dragged on her every inch of the way. Whatever moments she celebrated, I'm sure I ruined, or tried to. She soldiered on.

And then anguish. Not mine. Hers. I could feel it like it was inside me, too. How she must love me, or maybe by now it's loved. Past tense. I couldn't know. It didn't feel past tense. And what did she get in return? I hated myself and I wasn't even myself.

I never told her I loved her back in Nebraska, not to her face. And now, here in this version of California, I couldn't. I wanted to, but it wouldn't be right. I would be saying one kind of love, and she would hear another.

Or would she?

The question stopped me cold. Then it went deep. Abby drew into sharp focus as the room around her was masked by haze. There she was, the mature grown-up version of the mature youth from so many years ago. Her voice. Her mannerisms. So very familiar and so very strange. She was in control and she was good at it, which made her even more handsome. Firehose. I felt myself drawn across the unfocused room. High voltage wires, underground, again. Closer and closer. High voltage wires, unearthed. I wanted her. I wanted to disappear in her and let her make the stupid go away. Abby looked up and straight into my eyes. She knew. So did Black Lipstick Girl.

"Ouch!"

It was me. I looked down to see coffee draining from my cup and onto the front of my pants and then to the floor. The heads at the table swingarmed my way. Abby's head turned down. The staff sized up the situation. There was that crackle of anticipation. I think I was supposed to throw the cup now.

"It's nothing," I said.

Saucer eyes again and then heads swingarming back as I turned into the kitchen. Abby's eyes escorted me. I leaned on the counter, head dangling, out of breath. Eyes fixed on my unbroken pinky. What was I doing? Why did I want to be here? Why do I pity a person who isn't real? Well, she is real. She used to be real. I hope she is still real somewhere. Or is she real right now? I love her, but I don't love her like that, except I do. But I love my wife. My real wife, who I know is real. God in Heaven, I hope she's real. How on earth could I feel guilty about something I haven't done in a place where I am not? What do I want? What do I want? What, for God's sake, do I want?

"Dad?" Jennifer at the door. My hallucination daughter exhibiting very real concern. A rush in my chest. What was it? Something very familiar. Too familiar. The same rush of affection I felt when I beheld Mitt and Annie in real-life Atlanta.

Another rush to the chest. This one panic. Had I been talking out loud? Glance at Jennifer. Yes. Too loud? No. If that were the case, Abby would be there.

Detective mode. What had Jennifer heard? Time for some misdirection. How do you fake pain in your groin without attracting attention to your groin? You writhe, just so.

"Whoa, they, we brew the coffee hot here."

I watched Jennifer – apparently never Jenny or Jen – as I said it. Lame, but she seemed to buy it. She looked around.

"Who were you talking to?"

"Myself. I was angry at myself. The coffee. The spill."

"Okay."

Sunrise smile as she flitted back into the main room.

Sixteen. You can shrug it off so effortlessly at sixteen.

106

Sixteen. You know, you can only pretend a true thing isn't true until it gets real personal – especially if you can't even see it or touch it.

Sixteen. "Dad?" Personal. There to be seen. I felt that full body unfastening you get when you accept a truth, even if it's dreadful.

You disconnect from the illusion and exhale. It floats away and the truth settles in its place, where it should have been all along.

Sixteen. *"Oh, for God's sake, Matt...there...isn't...going...to be...a...baby."*

Which, finally, I knew was the root of the silent whisper in my head that had made me need to return to this whatever state. It wasn't Abby. Well, it was Abby, but it wasn't about Abby. It was Jennifer.

Sixteen. From the first second I saw her and knew she was of me. Sixteen. Which is also why I wanted so badly to leave and yet had to remain.

Sixteen. When the truth settles in place, it must be confronted as a truth. The illusion won't return. *"There...isn't... going...to be...a...baby."*

Exhale the illusion. The truth, you breathe it in.

Jennifer. What was the truth? Wherever I was, I wasn't in Nebraska anymore.

Jennifer – not Jenny or Jen – has a name. It changes everything. My hallucination daughter has a name.

And that was my burden. Sixteen years ago: *'As far as you're concerned, what happened back there never happened. It's like you were never there.'*

Today: Oh, yes you were.

A light touch on my arm made me spill coffee again. It was

no longer hot.

"You've been standing here forever."

It was Abby. Her voice held that blend of tenderness and disquiet and fixedness that came through when she knew I needed a cornerstone. "The meeting's over."

I didn't lift my head. She couldn't make the stupid go away. Nothing could. I was in the stupid. I *was* the stupid. The high voltage wires hummed. I didn't realize I was out of breath until I spoke.

"Jennifer, she's ours. Ours."

"Well, yes. Of course."

She touched my arm again. I drew back, even as I wanted her touch to remain. Instantly, I knew I hurt her. Again. Just like yesterday in the car, if there even was a yesterday. She started to leave the doorway. I breathed out the words.

"No. I mean, it's not, it's not what you think. Please stay."

And then I could see Gray, leaning back and creaking in his swivel chair, baton in motion: "So, it's 'now what?' for you. Which one are you? The new foundation or the old?"

"I thought I'd done that," I said to the kitchen counter below me.

"Done what?" Abby's voice toggled me from the daydream to the moment. I was way past detective mode or misdirection. I tried the truth.

"I'm useless to you and I'm a jerk. And I'm tired."

"I didn't know you were tired."

Abby. She always pounced when she sensed self-pity. But the cornerstone was still in her voice. "We're done. Let's go."

I didn't move.

"And you aren't useless," she said. "Just when everybody is sick of your drivel, you say something brilliant."

My eyes traveled to the magazine clipping. Abby's followed. She gave me an eyeroll.

"You should never have closed the door to your office when she was here."

Ardent. Charming. Another one. Must be a long line.

With that, she left. The door stayed vacant for maybe a millionth of a second before it filled with Black Lipstick Girl, silent as fog.

"Tomorrow," she said.

I gave her my I-need-more look.

"Tomorrow, you know. Tomorrow."

This time like she was talking to a child. This moment, whatever it was, needed to go away.

"Tomorrow," I said it in neutral. No meaning attached. Must have been enough. She warmed and bounced away, like she was skipping. Then she stopped.

In the Mondrian room, a voice raised in anger. And I mean raised. I knew the squeak. I pulled my head up. Abby was near the table with her you-can't-make-this-stuff-up look. Black Lipstick Girl didn't move. I walked around her.

There was Jeremiah Mora, all ablack and waving a piece of paper. Next to him was a gray suit. Colorless. Pinstripes. I guessed there was a man inside it. To the side of them was our staff, now standing. I approached as the staff swingarmed until we were in a little cluster. Now everybody could watch.

Jeremiah held out the piece of paper and sniffed.

"Did you bring this for me?" I said. "How nice."

I couldn't help it. Gray was right. I am a work in progress. Jeremiah started to bull up, then his eyes went half-lidded and he looked away. Time to see what was afoot. I read my piece of paper.

It was a bill for a million dollars. I showed it to Abby while Jeremiah awaited the meltdown he didn't get. Abby had her here-we-go-again look.

"What did you do?"

"I stood on a block of granite."

Jeremiah went Vesuvius. It was a squeaky eruption.

"It is not granite. That's the whole point."

How much anguish can you put into the word "whole?" I don't know what the limit is, but old buddy Jeremiah tore the word right out of himself. So, I had to ask.

"Well, what is it?"

Eruption two. He started to bounce up and down. "You know what it is." Anguish again on the word "know." "Twenty-three, Sixty-nine, Five is plastic that looks like granite. It represents a void. It is a presence that's really an absence. That's the statement."

He sputtered while I gave him time to finish off his insult. It came. "Philistine!"

"Who's this," I said, pointing at the suit.

"My attorney," said Jeremiah. He stepped back, crossed his arms and gave the suit the go-ahead.

The suit stepped up and handed me a card. There it was. Proof. He was an attorney, or at least he had an attorney's card, at least that's what I assumed, having not actually read it, that it was an attorney's card. The suit began to speak. I didn't listen. I couldn't listen. While he droned, I fixed my eyes on Jennifer, whose flashing eyes were fixed on the suit.

There it was. The mix. My Nebraska fury bridled by Abby's temperance. The cool reined the heat. I couldn't take my eyes off her. Why? Because it was real. You can't imagine something like that. You can't dream in that focus. The mix. You have to see it to grasp it, and I saw it.

I felt like I'd just thrown off another anvil. This moment was real and I'd always known it. It was just a matter of admitting it. That it was also thoroughly impossible still didn't seem to matter.

Sixteen years. The mix. Now what?

I spoke, not taking my eyes off Jennifer. I didn't know, and I didn't care, if I interrupted the suit. "Look, I tried to apologize for this yesterday."

The sound of another something dropping. Apparently, I don't apologize. "But now I've changed my mind."

I took my eyes off Jennifer and turned to Jeremiah.

"What was the name of it. Sixty-five, Twenty…"

"Twenty-three, Sixty-nine, Five."

He actually reached a higher note on that one. Almost a scream.

"Right. Well, you have a lot in common with your work." This one put Mora off balance. Everybody else was silent. "Your presence creates a void, too."

Mora tried to get his brain around this. You could see the cogs turning. I didn't wait. It was time to end this song and dance and go Nebraska on this guy.

"If I scratched your non-granite black plastic box, well, that validates the statement, doesn't it? I enhanced your work."

Somewhere in the hapless mind of Jeremiah Mora, the cogs were spinning faster. Connections were being made. More cogs. Littler ones. And more, until they formed a little cog troop, all a-working. I held up the bill.

"I think I made Twenty-three, Sixty-nine, Five worth a million and one dollars," I said. "You owe me a buck."

And then, there it was, the thousand-yard stare. Dead air. Jeremiah Mora would have to recover before squeaking again. I decided to fill the time.

"And by the way, just how did I scratch the thing?"

"With this," it was the voice of the colorless suit, but a different voice. Smoky and sandpapery and familiar. I watched his hand – the now too familiar shades of black and white substituting for flesh tones – open to reveal a fifty-cent piece.

The hand tossed the coin my way.

It flipped in the air. I caught it. I opened my palm.

Heads.

VI
HEADS

All interstate highways look alike in the dark, at least if you are standing on the shoulder of one. No Man's Land. Constant roar. Rushing and whooshing. A death threat only feet away.

The electric moment retreated from my brain. The familiar chillbumps faded. The lights went from a blur to a stream. I could only hope I was in Atlanta. My pinky was bent. Even in the dark, I could tell my clothes weren't black. So far, so good.

In the glare of his headlights, I couldn't tell if the man before me was an Atlanta cop. I could tell he was a cop. Telltale red and blue flashers from his car washed color over him and the remnants of snow at his feet. His face was dark behind the beam of his flashlight.

Detective mode. Whatever I'd done, there were no pistols drawn. Felt like early evening. Hard to tell in the too-short days of winter.

When you are a cartoonist, you become an observer. There are moments when you distance yourself, whether you want to or not. It becomes built-in. You become alert to the staging and body language of life. You observe that people walking into restaurants have an entirely different body persona than people walking out. You know a man has a liquor bottle in the bag just by the way he holds it. You can spot the kid who broke the lamp by the way he stands there. You come to understand that body language can say stupid, but it can't say smart. You record it somewhere in your brain so you can use it later. You will recapture it to draw moments that your viewers can instantly grasp – "Ah, that guy's been pulled over by a cop."

He'd gotten me out of a car. I looked at it. Yes, it was my car. So, there was an odd comfort. At least I knew what I was in. I just didn't know where.

The cop looked up from my driver's license.

"Where's the fire?"

I guess they run out of original questions after a while. Still, it was a tough question. Brain search. Nothing, but he wanted something. I went for the truth. It came out.

"I…I just want to get home to my family."

This one brought the cop out of standard cop mode. His face changed in the flashlight half-light. Must have been the naked yearning in my voice. Somebody needed to say something. I picked me.

"I'm sorry."

I meant it. You could tell he knew I meant it. He just didn't know why. Sorrow. So much of it. Hanging on me like wet clothes. The cold non-real reality of what I'd left behind. He aimed the flashlight back toward my license.

"You the cartoonist? That Matt Andrews?"

Gratitude. I was in Atlanta.

New detective mode. If you are an honest cartoonist, sooner or later you pop everybody's bubble. Nobody gets left out. If you are good, people come to admire you for it. If you aren't good, you just irritate everyone. I never had a thing about the police. Tough job. But I always felt the first trait that might disqualify anyone from becoming a cop might be the desire to be a cop. Brain search. The file drawers opened one by one. No bad cop 'toons. I went with the legal answer.

"Guilty."

He flicked off his flashlight and handed me the license. "You piss off the same people I do. Go home."

He turned toward his car. It didn't seem like a good idea to ask him what day this was.

He stopped and spoke over his shoulder. "A few minutes isn't going to make a difference." He didn't use his cop voice. "They'll still be there."

He turned back and evaporated into the beams of his headlights.

They'll still be there. That was the question. Will they? There at the West Coast ad agency, I had been confident of my ability to return. Now, the swagger was gone. Return to what? I didn't know. There was too much I didn't know, but now I did know why I was doing 70.

I checked the clock in my car. This was my normal drive time home, but I never used the interstate. Our house was maybe ten blocks from downtown. I sometimes think I was the first person in Atlanta to commute by bicycle. The trip home was a simple drive down Piedmont, then a right and a left. Time to sort this out.

The cityscape grew familiar. The next exit sign told me exactly where I was. Home wasn't far. I navigated my way there.

I had a place and time. All I needed was the day.

Deja vu. I was back on the sidewalk in front of my house,

just like yesterday. Fading snow all around, just like yesterday. I yearned to enter my own house, just like yesterday. I was afraid to enter my own house, just like yesterday.

You know you are loved when you know that you are anticipated. When you walk through a door and you realize that your arrival, this moment, is the best part of someone else's day. There's nothing like it. Annie hugging my knees. Jill kissing my cheek. Mitt…well, Mitt's happy because everyone else is happy. I kissed Jill long and full. No firehose required. At length Jill pulled back, eyes a little sparkly.

She looked me over. "You didn't bring it."

Detective mode. Obviously, I had been given a swingby, as in, "can you swing by the store on the way home?" This was good. I was on record as failing to recall at least half of my swingby orders, and make no mistake, they were orders despite the question mark.

"Oops," my standard answer. "What was it again?"

"Wine and peanut butter."

A list only a parent could love.

"I'll go back out." Now that I knew home was home and I was on time, more or less, I also knew I could use some time to sort things out. "I'll take Annie."

You could tell even back then that it was just a matter of time before Atlanta had Third World traffic. Too many cars, too little concrete. But the congestion had thinned and the trip to the store – Annie strapped in and bubbling behind me – was easy enough.

Time to take stock. The questions. It seemed final. Whatever this is or was, isn't and wasn't a hallucination. What was it? As near as I could tell the Atlanta me was here when I was there – there being Los Angeles. Meanwhile, the Los Angeles me, the loathsome me, was in Los Angeles all the time. He never came to Atlanta. I, me, the Atlanta me, took his place when I appeared there. The bad me returned to Los Angeles me when I departed.

So, who took my place in Atlanta when I went to Los Angeles? Apparently, it was an Atlanta version of me who behaved like me. All I knew was that time didn't stop when I switched sides. Life went on. When I left Atlanta, nothing changed. There was work, family and swingbys. When I left Los Angeles, there was…what? What was my loathsome Los Angeles self up to when I wasn't there?

It's funny how things that are fearful, even inexplicable, can become reassuring when they grow familiar. The colorless hands. The fifty-cent piece. The flip. The electric rush. The goosebumps. My broken or unbroken pinky and nose. My wardrobe change. They all circled around in my head until they found homes.

By the time Annie and I made our way back up our sidewalk, I felt oddly normal. The reassuring things seemed to outweigh the questions, mostly because the questions were unanswerable, especially the big one. Was any of this real? For even that, I had half an answer. I'd decided for the second time in Los Angeles that whatever this was, it was real enough.

It was also strangely comforting that I had come to know, and perhaps understand, the loathsome Los Angeles me. It was like he was arrested in time the night I drove around that corner in Nebraska. While I went on to be nurtured by Gray, the loathsome me remained forever adolescent and raw and self-seeking. He became famous for a painting. A painting I'm sure he couldn't paint. Abby was still his crutch. She was still, with the exception of Jennifer, the only person who could stand him. He was an older, unfledged version of the Nebraska me and on his way to becoming a full-grown warthog.

I couldn't stand him, but there was no denying who he was – me.

But here in Atlanta he wasn't me, or at least he wasn't here and maybe he didn't exist at all. Comforting. Strange. And then Jill, Annie, Mitt and me, the Atlanta us. We spent a conventional, middle class evening together. It was like heaven. No. It *was* heaven.

I didn't live in a real world and a hallucination. I lived in two realities.

VII
DAY THREE

You could just see the nose, soda-bottle glasses and hair-crazed forehead of Joel from the newspaper morgue. All else was covered by the books and boxes of clippings in his arms. You could tell from those eyes, though, that he was excited. I had sent him right up his alley.

I had rushed through the morning gauntlet with Farley. I found that it was quicker if I was deferential and pretended to be in a great hurry. This time he didn't retreat through his door. I phoned Joel with an order for anything he could dig up concerning time travel and extrasensory perception. I also put him on the hunt for a woman named Abby Andrews – not Alexander – a 16-year old named Jennifer Andrews, and a firm called Andrews Advertising. Try California first. I was fairly sure they wouldn't show up, but I had to know.

I cleared a space on my desk so Joel could pile his load there.

He grabbed two books and thrust them at me. "These are the best ones." Setting them down, he grabbed a third. "This one after them."

I leafed through them. Joel's name was written inside the

covers. These weren't morgue reference books. They were from Joel's personal library on the paranormal.

I put them aside. Way too much to absorb quickly. "What about the people?

"No Abby Andrews or Jennifer Andrews that fit your age description. No ad agency. Here are the only clippings, but not even close."

No surprise. As I returned to the books, I realized Joel was watching me intently. He was itching to speak, and he did.

"It's real, you know. ESP. Sixth Sense. Second Sight." He sat down. This was a first. Joel never sat. He was always on his way somewhere.

"Telepathy, the study of it, is a hundred years old. People today say it is fraud, but it's part of every culture and goes way, way back to prophecy. It happens in life. You can't just make it happen in a lab."

He adjusted his glasses. He was just warming up.

"Time travel. That goes way back, too, to Hindu mythology. It's in the Jewish tradition and in Japanese tales. It's not just H.G. Wells."

I gave him my I-get-it look. He needed it. Joel needed to know I wasn't poking fun at him, even though he knew I took him seriously every day. There was more.

"And bilocation. Being in two places at once. That goes back to Greek Mythology."

I gave him my I-get-it look again.

"These people," he pointed to the box of clippings. "These people you are looking for, do you know them? Family?"

Joel rarely asked questions. He came. He delivered. He went. He deserved an answer.

I gave him the best honest answer I could. "Yes and no."

120

Joel nodded.

One thing you could say about Joel. He understood ambiguity.

"Thanks for all this," I said. "Lots of work to do."

Joel rose and made for the door. He was almost through it when he piled back in.

"It's called the Quantum Robin." The words rushed from him. He was dead serious and had my attention. "It's also called 'entanglement.'"

I motioned him back to the chair. He sat – if you want to call bouncing and twitching sitting – on the edge.

"Einstein called it 'spooky action at a distance.' Two or more electrons are linked to each other even when separated by long distances. No physical connection. It also works in the magnetic sensory organs of birds and animals. It was actually proven after his death, Einstein's I mean, and only just recently. Bilocation is real. But it's not new. Magnetism. Magnesium."

He was just warming up.

"The Titans Cronus and Rhea were pretty much the beginning of Greek mythology. Cronus was the Titan of time. Rhea the Titan of fertility."

I gave him my now-you-lost-me look.

"Every time Rhea gave birth to a child, Cronus devoured it whole."

I gave him my where-is-this-going look.

"When Zeus was born, Rhea substituted a rock in his blanket. Cronus swallowed the rock, and Zeus was saved."

I gave him my wrap-it-up look.

"The rock was magnesium. Magnesium comes from the stars. It's also in our bodies. It is also essential to every cell. The Greeks knew. Magnetism. Attraction from a distance. It's in us."

He said the last words slowly, watching my eyes. I got up and closed the door, then gave him my tell-me-more look. He did.

"Yesterday, you asked me if you were all here Monday. You weren't. I mean, you were physically here. Here. But you were just going through the motions."

"When? What part of the day?"

"The afternoon. After lunch."

"What do you mean 'just going through the motions?'"

"I mean your mind was…elsewhere. I can't really describe it."

"Like a trance?"

"No. Like somebody who had too much to think about."

"Was I me, I mean, otherwise? Or did I change?"

"Yes. I mean, no. You didn't change. You were you. Just quieter. Same thing happened Monday. I know because I talked with you. Tried to, anyway."

I went deep into my brain. Nothing. No explanation. I was me, but I was half there. For a moment, I forgot Joel was there.

"Were you in, uh, Los Angeles?"

The question brought me back into the room.

"Why do you ask?"

He pointed to the Jeremiah Mora clipping on my board. "Well, that's where all these come from. Did you meet him two days ago? Or yesterday."

I didn't bother to consider my answer. "Yes and no. And both days."

Joel wouldn't take his eyes off mine. He was waiting for more. He knew there was more. He stood up and sat down. He rose for good. He was no longer the sixth-floor errand boy. I wasn't sure what to give him, so I gave him the lead.

"I'm not an electron."

122

"But you were in two places. Two places at one time."

"I don't think so. I don't remember being here."

"But I remember you being here."

He let this sink in. I let it sink in. His pager went off. He ignored it. I ignored it. He had a question. You could tell he had a question.

"How does it happen?"

Until that moment, I'd never fully considered it. I took stock of myself and the room as it dawned on me that Joel might be the only person on the planet to whom I could fully disclose this whole thing, whatever it was. I thought out loud as I pieced it together.

"With a flip of a coin."

Joel's eyes started moving. You could tell he was searching his mental encyclopedia of arcana. I gave him more.

"It's a fifty-cent piece. It has no color. I mean, it's not even silver. It's black and white, like old television. So is the hand that holds it and flips it."

"All you see is the hand?"

"When the coin is out, it's all I look at."

"So, the hand belongs to a person you never see."

"Well, yeah, but only because I don't look. And it's never the same person. Well, it's the same person, but in different ways. Different roles or personas. He – it's always a 'he' – just shows up."

"Do you know him?"

"We've never met. I don't even know if he's real. He has a rough voice. Peculiar."

"Do other people notice him?"

This got my attention.

"No. Just me." I'm sure Joel could hear the revelation in my voice. "The hand flips the coin. If it's tails, I go to Los Angeles. If it's heads, I come here. Atlanta."

"At the same time? I mean hour, time of day."

"Yes, even with the time change it works out." I decided to go all in. He might as well hear it all. "But not the same me."

Joel's pager went off again. He flicked it off and disengaged it.

"What do you mean, 'not the same me?'"

Where to begin? Who had the time for the full story? I decided Joel did. His pager would be silent. "Remember Farley telling you I was a juvenile delinquent?"

"He said it again yesterday."

"Well, I was, and worse. But something, someone, a special person, changed me. Okay, I changed myself, but I couldn't have done it without him. That changed person, that's the me who is here with you right now. The me in Los Angeles never changed. He's the adult version of the juvenile and still a delinquent."

"Janus." The word breathed out of Joel as he rose from his chair.

Janus, I knew. Mythological god with two faces.

"Janus," he said again, with more force. "God of time, duality, journeys, transitions and passages, beginnings and endings. Roman. There is no Greek version."

We went quiet. Joel was under his own spell. I was putting puzzle pieces together in my brain. The silence broke with a loud knock on the door. Actually, many knocks. You could call it pounding. Then, the unwelcome voice of E. Farley Haman.

"Joel! I know you're in there!" Joel rose and opened the door as wide as his face. "Joel, I've been paging you."

"Sorry, mister...doctor Haman. Must be my batteries."

Joel slipped out. He didn't glance back.

Janus. Time, duality and journeys. Beginnings and endings. Attraction from a distance. I filed this away in the ever-growing warehouse section of my head that housed the incidents of the last 48-plus hours. Other than the obvious, there was something else bothering me to the core about the last few days.

It was control, or, actually, the absence of it.

I was being controlled. Controlled by a coin. No, controlled by a man flipping a coin. A man who seemed to have no color. A nameless, faceless man. A stranger with a peculiar voice. Here's what I did know – I had to wrest back control.

But of what? Time. Duality. Distance. Journeys. Beginnings and endings. How about crazy? Here I was starring in my own nutshow. Or was it a nutshow? Actual or unreal, my desire to control it was very real.

And then, Joel. Joel. He bought the whole thing. You could tell. He didn't for a moment question my sanity.

I tugged out my fifty-cent piece. Yeah, I had one. Do you know how hard it was to find a fifty-cent piece in 1980? I had to buy gum in four places before a clerk scraped one out of the register. I didn't flip the coin. I was sure I never would.

Fear. No, control.

Control. That was it.

Or maybe it was something far deeper. Only yesterday, I had admitted to myself that I wasn't in a hallucination or a nutshow. What I experienced in Los Angeles was real.

Here is where it went deep. So were the feelings. The queasy non-guilt guilt that came over me when I firehosed Abby away. The sparkle of Jennifer's touch on my hand, a parent's hand. Neither went away when I returned to Atlanta, even if Atlanta was heaven.

I had two families. It didn't matter if I was the only person on Earth who knew it. Janus. Two faces. How about splitting in two? When I was in Los Angeles, I yearned to come home. When I was with my Atlanta family, I couldn't suppress diversions of mind. Diversions to Los Angeles. The mystery. What was going on with the dreadful me while I was away?

Was I being dishonest? With who? Jill, Annie and Mitt? Abby and Jennifer? Myself? How can you be dishonest if you don't even know if what you are doing is real?

But it was real. I kept circling around it. Yesterday, Los Angeles was real. Today, it's not. Joel brought the evidence, or lack of it. There was no denying it, but my sense of dishonesty was concrete. Real. Honesty. That was it.

No, it wasn't. And finally, it went full depth. There almost certainly was a real Abby in my Atlanta world. I just didn't know where she was. But was there a Jennifer? *"There…isn't…going…to be…a…baby."* What if there was?

Sixteen. A Jennifer out there somewhere. Jennifer with a sunrise smile. This was a very real possibility and one I'd turned my back on so long ago.

Sixteen. It doesn't seem so long in the grand scheme of things.

Control.

Imagine an empty field. Now imagine you drive a post into the ground at a certain spot in the field. It could be any spot. Side, middle, back, whatever. It changes the entire field. Anything that enters the field is relative to the post. It's in front of the post, behind the post, north of the post, south, near, far, next to it. The post subdues the field.

It's the same on paper. Every drawing begins with a stroke. Every stroke that follows must be in accord with the first one. I don't know how many sheets of paper marked with a single stroke I've wadded and tossed, let's just say plenty. That's your brain signaling you aren't in the drawing zone yet. You haven't seized what awaits you.

Now, I faced the same problem, but life isn't sketched on paper. To seize what awaited me in these dual realities I had to make my first stroke. I had to plant my post in the field and work from there. How? I didn't know where to start. The blank remained a blank. Empty. A lacuna.

A knock on my door. It opened. Joel peeked in. His eyes went directly to the fifty-cent piece in my hand. I tossed it to him as he entered. He snatched it with equal parts fear and anticipation.

"Don't worry. I don't think two people go on a flip," I said. "Besides, it doesn't work if you flip it yourself. I don't think so, anyway. So far, it's gotta be that other guy."

You could tell Joel had something on his mind, but I was too deep in multiple self-revelations. Still, I wanted him in the room. He eyed the coin. Then me. "Farley told me not to come back in here."

"Bad boy."

"I just want you to know I'm not the one who gave it to him. Wasn't me."

"Gave him what?"

"That town in Nebraska. Your old town. Not the Missouri town on your resume."

"So, you were right. Farley is bird-dogging me."

"He's working with the equivalent of me at the local paper there. The morgue librarian."

At that moment, the real Abby may as well have been in the room. She was so present in my mind. If there was a real Jennifer, Farley would try to find her. If there wasn't a real

Jennifer, Farley would try to find out why. I looked up at Joel.

"How do you know?"

"He has a letter on his desk. I read it upside down."

"You can do that?"

"Sure. The Nebraska librarian said she's still looking for more information on 'the incident.'"

Joel eyed me. I didn't give him much back. There were so many incidents, but only one that mattered. Joel went on. He more or less said what was going to be my next thought. I don't know how he did it.

"This person. This person who changed you. Have you talked to him about, you know, about this?" He gestured with the fifty-cent piece.

"No. You are the only person who knows any of this."

"Would he understand?"

"He would try to."

"Then why haven't you called him?"

Bam. Brain alert. This was way too obvious. Gray Jarvis would be the post in the field.

"I will." I reached for the phone.

"But you can't."

"I can't?"

"You have to call him from the other side of the coin."

I gave Joel my hold-the-phone look as I, well, as I held the phone. This was obvious, too. If I approached Gray as the East Coast me that he knew, where would we go from there? I'd tell him the story. He'd listen. Then what? If I came to him as the West Coast me, I would for the first time put the two realities together, more or less.

I wouldn't call Gray.

When – make that if – I was flipped again, I'd go see him.

128

Goosebumps. Then a creepy feeling and goosebumps again. When. When. There was no if.

I knew I'd be flipped again. Knew it. Sooner or later. I replaced the goosebumps with Gray's presence in my thoughts. Yes, Gray would try, but even if he couldn't grasp the whole thing like Joel, he could guide me. He could help me make some sense of the known realities. Realities to me. The two families. The dishonesty. The possibility. Answers. Gray would have answers. I looked up to see Joel still responding to my hold-the-phone look.

"Did you just go? I mean, did you just, just flip?" He bit his lip.

"I was caught up in my thoughts."

Joel shrank about two inches when he exhaled. "We need something. I need a way to maybe know if I'm talking to the real you or the absent you. Right then, I thought maybe I was talking to the absent you."

He leveled his eyes at me. You could tell he was still unsure.

I gave reassurance a shot. "I never flip without the presence of that coin."

"But you said other people don't notice the Black and White Man. What if he's, you know, invisible to me?"

"No," I said, "It only occurs in normal routine settings. The only way I could flip now is if you were or if you became the Black and White Man."

Became. That's what happened with the attorney in the suit at Abby's studio. He became the Black and White Man.

More goosebumps. Creepy goosebumps. And then I found out what paranoia feels like. Did the Black and White Man appear on his own while nobody could see him? Nobody?

Joel had already put the two thoughts together. He carefully, very carefully, held the fifty-cent piece away from him like a dead cat. He carefully, very carefully, came to me and placed it in my palm without turning it over.

I watched every tiny slow-motion moment of this. Fear. Then nothing. Just crazy. I shook my head. The crazy had to stop. This was Joel. Joel from the morgue. Good old Joel. The goosebumps faded, and Joel's pager went off.

He glanced at it and shifted toward the door. "We still need something."

"Your pager," I said. "I'll page you from the flip side. I know your number. It will stay with me. If you get a long-distance page, it's me."

Joel nodded and he was gone. He didn't say, "Then what?"

✳✳✳

It was happening again and I didn't like it. The push and pull. The night before, in the dark on the interstate, you couldn't have made me return to the Loathsome West Coast Me at gunpoint. Only minutes ago, dread at the thought. Now, minutes later, here I was twisting my own desire all over again.

I should go back. Gray. Yes. Why yes? I didn't know.

Yes, I did.

Aside from my parents, Gray was the only person I could contact who knew the old me and the new me. That's what this was all about, wasn't it? The old me a rock' n roll warthog in L.A.?

Okay, I did want to go back. I did want Gray to see the warthog. Why? That one I didn't know. Maybe just to complete the circle. He saw the boy. Now he could see the man, except I wouldn't really be that man. I'd be me. He could assess me. I sensed my own vanity coming into play. Enough.

Enough of this. I had a workday to wrap up.

I had already pulled a 'toon from the sick day file. It was an evergreen and not really all that lame, considering. I would deliver the thing to the engraving department myself and then head home. Farley could remark tomorrow that I again left early.

Elevators. You always want them to be crowded or empty. You don't want three or less in the little cube. Something would need to be said and there was not enough time for anything that wasn't stupid. The doors slid open. We would be two. I had an elevator partner, five floors to go.

Eyes down. I decided to fold in on myself and play the thoughts in my head.

So, E. Farley Haman was close to getting the goods on me. A librarian in Nebraska. An incident.

Incident. A trifling word. What incident?

What if Farley uncovered my story? Did I care? To begin with, I didn't know what my story was. I knew what was a matter of record. I was in trouble and plenty of it when I was a kid.

I pulled the fifty-cent piece and pretended to examine it. Quantum Robin. Bilocation. Janus. Attraction.

"You don't see those much anymore," the sandpaper voice, now familiar, too familiar, unfolded me. "Lemme have a look."

I knew there was no point in attempting to move. I was anchored, rigid and numb. I watched as the colorless hand nicked the coin from my palm without touching me. I watched the hand hold it in front of my eyes, two fingers moving it back and forth, revealing both sides.

Slow motion. The hand slipped the coin back in my palm. Tails.

VIII
TAILS

Tell me I don't own a pair of silk boxer shorts.
Make that black silk.

The rush passed, and the thrill and tingle faded. Familiar
sequence now. The static in my ears would soon dissolve. The
disembodied voices would calm. My eyes would clear. The
anchor would go away, and I would be released into the other
side. And there I was.

Usually, I checked my broken finger first, but the boxers won
my attention. Would I ever stop discomfiting myself?

Voice. Female voice. Young female voice. I was not alone.
In black silk boxers. I had yet another daytime drink in my
unbroken pinky hand. I looked toward the voice.

Black Lipstick Girl on a bed in a room. Of course. My West
Coast luck, it had to be. She was covered to the shoulders by
sheets, trying too hard to be coquettish. Her manner seemed
rehearsed. She was expectant. Whatever was going on, it was my
move.

Detective mode. I hadn't expected to know the room and I
didn't. It was oddly precious and flouncy. Little girlish without

133

the dolls. Wallpaper, cute little apple trees. Her lipstick wasn't smudged. I ran my finger across my lips. No lipstick, so I guessed no contact so far unless she made herself up and got back in bed, which I considered a possibility in her case.

"This must be tomorrow."

Whatever she expected from me, it wasn't that. Her face fell. Her face. She wore the vacancy of youth like makeup. Why Abby hired her wasn't coming through. Then again, maybe Abby didn't hire her. A thought came. I could fix this. I could change the outcome of things in this world. I could make it better even if I didn't know if it existed at all. Also, I wanted to get out. Fast.

"We're not doing this," I said.

She shifted under the sheets. No need for a firehose.

A quick search for my shirt. I knew to look for black. Floor. There it was. With my black pants.

"But you said…"

"I don't care what I said."

Shirt half on and counting.

"We're not doing this. Now or ever again. Whatever this is, it's over."

"Whatever this is?"

There it was – actually, there it wasn't – in her voice. All ire. No hurt. She didn't care about me, the West Coast me, the loathsome me. This wasn't about affection. This was a transaction. I don't think I was supposed to know that.

"What did you think?" I said. Shirt buttoned, I kicked the pants from the floor up to my hands. "We'd become a permanent item? You would move into Abby's place?"

It was a guess, but it was dead on. Her face lost its vacancy. A slideshow of emotions crossed it until the final slide stuck. She looked cornered. She started to speak until I gave her my don't-even-think-about-it look.

Pants at knees and counting.

"I don't know why Abby hired you."

Black Lipstick Girl didn't challenge that. Abby did hire her.

"So, you must be good at what you do."

She smiled to herself. My pants, way too tight. Struggle and shimmy. Tuck the boxers. A hop and a zip.

"But however good you are, or think you are, you can't carry her shoes."

I must admit, part of me wanted that smile to go away. It did. Then the other part of me felt cruel, even though it was the truth.

Time for a little tenderness. I lowered the tone.

"Don't you understand? The agency isn't about me. It never was. Abby built it. Built it by herself."

I assumed this was true. Pretty easy to fill in the blanks on the story. Pretty sure the loathsome West Coast me wasn't much help.

"She knows talent. She sees something in you. Give it to her. Grow it."

Black Lipstick Girl sat up a bit. Every cartoonist knows posture speaks louder than thought balloons. The rehearsed coquette was gone. It was like she became herself right before my eyes. She almost matched the décor.

Gray Jarvis: "Where does capacity come from? How deep is depth? Why doesn't everyone have it? How is it that, so often, people who do have it don't know it? The first two questions are mysteries. Insoluble. The third question is also a mystery, but you can help people start, but only start, to solve it for themselves."

"What about you?" she said.

"We don't have enough time to talk about what I don't

know."

Shoes. Loafers. Good, I wouldn't have to waste time tying laces.

"Including where my car is."

And I was out the door. The car, my car, my gaudy car, was easy to find. It fairly shouted out there on the street.

I don't care who you are, driving an overpriced, overdesigned, overpowered car makes you smile, and I did.

This stopped me. I mean it really stopped me. I pulled over. Quick mirror check. And then I understood. Getting into that car was like trying on the old me. The silk boxers arrived on their own when I switched sides, but this, the car, was a choice. Well, sort of a choice. How else would I get away? But it didn't feel like a choice of necessity. My first flip stay in my odious West Coast house was a prison of loathing. No grins there, but here I was smiling. A car like this is made to feel like an extension of you, which is why I liked it in a perverse way, and I didn't like that I liked it, perverse or not. Which me was being extended? Maybe this was really why I wanted Gray to see me on this side. Was I becoming comfortable, too comfortable in this maybe-maybe not world? Was there room for happiness here, at least on my part, and what on earth could that mean? Did I want Gray to rescue me again? No. Of course not.

When you ask yourself if you are overthinking something, it means you are overthinking something. I spoke to my reflection in the mirror.

"Leave me alone."

I was driving to Andrews Advertising and how did I know the direction? The direction is all I knew, but I knew.

The full turn-by-turn directions I got from a gas station attendant. I gave him the street address. The address I remembered from the day before. It was on the door. I also got a map of the western United States.

I wouldn't fly to Missouri. Again and again, the thought had occurred to me. Again and again, I recoiled. I could see it. Me, walking the ramp to the plane, like I was entering a time capsule, getting on the plane in one world and getting off in another with a void in between. No. No. That was already happening to me without a ticket. Suffocating. Like a coffin. No way.

I needed to be grounded. I needed to look out the window and know that I could stop and step out and stand there and be in control. There it was again. Control. There would be no attendant telling me where to sit, no voice from a stranger coming over a speaker, "This is the cabin, our flight plans have changed." Control. Me.

I had a plan. What I didn't have, or wasn't sure I had, was time. So far, all my trips to this side could be measured in hours. I needed days. I had no control over Black and White Man and his terrible coin. I had a plan. Maybe I could outdrive him. I would drive to Missouri. I would meet with Gray. We would, he would, figure this whole thing out.

So, why was I driving to Andrews Advertising? If there had been a button on my forehead, it would have read "autopilot." I was driving to Andrews Advertising because I wanted to see Abby. Did I know she was there? No. Or maybe I did. Of course. Wanted? No. No, I needed to see her. No, that wasn't it. It was a responsibility. Crazy as it sounds, I would tell her that I wouldn't be in town.

The person who isn't actually her husband and wasn't actually there wouldn't be in town.

I wheeled onto the yellow-banded lava bed that provided the parking adjacent to Andrews Advertising. I was grateful to exit the car. By now, I was weary of the thing. It just tried too hard. It seemed...melancholy.

The glass door guillotined the traffic noise, and now, library-style silence. The absence of bustle. The presence of elaborate thought. The Mondrian space was empty. On the other side of the glass walls, the staff hunched over the drafting tables in their little rooms. Abby came out of hers, folders in hand.

I couldn't help it. I heard the music. She was genuinely shocked to see me. You could just tell.

"Well, look what the cat drug in."

No time for chit-chat. I went straight to it. "I'm...I'm just checking in."

"Checking in."

"Yes. Checking in. I'm going out of town."

She put down the folders. "You're going out of town and you're letting me know. Me."

"Yeah. You."

She gave me that look. The same one she gave me after I crawled into her house the first time. Part worry, part wary, part pleased. "Alone?"

"Yeah."

She watched my face. I watched hers. She believed me.

"Where are you going?"

I was ready for this one. I decided to just tell her. The truth was no stranger than any fiction I could cook up. "To Missouri."

The look again. "Missouri."

"Yeah. Missouri. I'm going to call on an old friend. You don't know him. I need to...I just need to see him."

"You have an old friend I don't know and he's a him."

"Name's Gray Jarvis. A preacher."

"A preacher." She tossed the folders on the meeting table.

"Let's go."

"Let's. Us?"

"Yup. You and a preacher. This I gotta see."

I wasn't prepared for this, to say the least. Recalculation. Delay. No way I could stop her. I might as well just stop worrying about the time. Abby went into her office and made a call, hustled back out and went into one of the other little glass and steel rooms, an empty one, and left a note. She swept back out and made for the door.

"You coming?"

"What about all this? The agency."

"Matt. If anything comes along Tilly will manage things. She's always wanted to."

"Who's Tilly?"

Oops. A blurt. A giveaway blurt. Abby gave me the look, this time minus the pleased part. Then I knew. Black Lipstick Girl had a name. Tilly. And Abby knew the truth about Tilly.

She turned toward the door. "You coming?"

I came.

The call Abby made from her office was to Jennifer. She had Abby's bags packed when we got to her house. Surprise, she'd packed her own bags, too.

I had followed Abby to her house in my overdesigned car. It was a two-seater. We would now go in Abby's car. She tossed her bags in the trunk and looked at me.

"Where's your luggage?"

Did I mention I had a plan?

It was incomplete.

"I don't have any."

It had been sixteen years since I'd gotten the I'm-tired-of-acting-like-your-mother look, but there it was. Abby followed it with a sigh and went into her house. Jennifer and I waited. Jennifer was excited but she didn't speak. Abby returned with a Dopp Kit and an overnight bag. She was quick about it.

"You'll still fit into these." She motioned with the bag. Then she gave me another look. Sly. "And none of it is black."

The old clothes I understood. At least I thought so. Mine from another time. The Dopp Kit? Did Abby have a boyfriend? Boyfriend. The word almost made me laugh. Boyfriend. With a toothbrush. Was this jealousy I was feeling? Firehose.

"Where are we going?" It was Jennifer, expectant.

"We're going to Missouri," I said.

"But first, we're going to the Grand Canyon," Abby said.

Jaw-dropper. The Grand Canyon.

Dismay. Queasiness.

I took Jill there on our honeymoon. We drove from Missouri – a long slow drive with room for talking – as the American West filled our windshield with promise. It's a magical place for anyone, but it was more than magic for Jill and me.

"What's wrong?" Abby yanked me back to my otherworldly present. "We can make it in about seven hours and it's about time you kept your promise."

So, I'd promised Abby a trip to the Grand Canyon, but that was a slow drive with room for talking that never happened. I found myself wondering what this world would look like if it had. Time to buy in.

"Sure. Let's go." I started for the driver's seat, but Abby beat me to it.

"Women in front. Men in back." Abby and Jennifer announced this together. No, they sang it. They were happy. Very happy.

I was unsettled. It all felt too good. Genuine. Like I should be there.

✳✳✳

Riding along in the back seat of a car is a great place to think. The people in front forget about you after a while. You just go away from their minds and settle into your own little world. Soon enough, we were over the mountains and beyond Los Angeles.

My thoughts were farther away. The Grand Canyon. A few more hours. Jill all those years ago. That long slow drive cemented us. We were two people before. We were one after.

I met Jill while I was working at the church before I went into the Navy. She was still there when I came back and she'd gone from a tomboy farm girl to the woman she is today.

I saw her again for the first time. I never had a chance after that.

I never went looking for a dance partner. When I was young and delinquent, the girls just came my way. Except for Abby, they all left. Fast. They all wanted me to care.

During my years of study and work at the little country church in Missouri, I was isolated at first and preferred things that way. I rarely went into town. I met only those who came on Sunday or dropped by for this or that.

This changed as the farmers on the surrounding prairie made it plain they accepted me. No, they welcomed me. They had that easy-going nature of people who knew what they are doing and why. Sooner than I could have expected, they were treating me like family. I didn't think about it much, just figured it was because I had the Gray Jarvis stamp of approval.

The girls – I guess they were women by then – were

141

courteous, if a little distant. I was a repair project. Everybody knew it and that was fine by me.

Like the others, Jill was courteous and distant. Looking back, though, it seemed she was around more. Lingering here. Showing up there. Helping out and knowing when help was needed. She was around enough that I became comfortable with her, at least more comfortable than with any others. It was only a matter of time before I knew I wanted her to linger. I wanted her to show up. I wanted her to help out. I wanted her to speak. It was a slow lightning strike, but it landed. When it came time for me to speak, I was only half tongue-tied. I know that's a mixed metaphor. I don't care. It's how it was.

She had a face you could look into for a long time. At first glance it was so imperfect, and then it reconfigured itself into perfection while you watched. She was dignified and approachable at the same time. She was kind and she was firm. She saw humor. Her common sense ran deep. She was perceptive. She could put things together. Add all this to the domestic and trade skills that come refined in a farm kid and you have competence with a polished surface. You have a complete person.

She didn't blink when I told her I would draw cartoons for a living. I think she was sure it would happen while I was still wondering if it would, or how. She did blink when Atlanta happened. It was so sudden. Then it was obvious to us both. She would go, too.

I've been around long enough now to know that I had it easy.

Easy. No, that's not the right word. It was straightforward. Jill in the churchyard waiting for me. I didn't have to look anywhere else. I know it can be hard to find a dance partner if you're looking. Where do you start? Or does it start itself? Why her? Why me?

Gray: "The hardest person to know is yourself. That's because you think you do know yourself. You've told yourself all about yourself. Everything is explained! Then it isn't, and you are lost. When no mirror works, you have to look inside. 'Who am I, really?'"

The dance. Your partner. The one who gets inside. You move. You adjust. You feel. You get lost in who is who, even when you aren't together. That was Jill. Sometimes it was like her voice was my own voice talking – make that singing – to me.

You've gotta hear the music.

And there it was. There in the back seat. Alone but not alone. For the first time in this side of the coin, I didn't carry those jimjam, gotta get back, cold creeps. I had a plan. I would get answers. Jill could understand, or would understand, or did understand, wherever she was. Whatever this was.

They say when you are confronted with your mortality, your life passes before your eyes. I guess the same thing happens in a car in the desert. It was my own little home movie. Jill and me. Our little wedding in the gazebo at Gray's church. Driving across the country to the Grand Canyon. Moving to Atlanta. Me telling her about E. Farley Haman. Her fretting that I'd be confrontational. Me guaranteeing her I would be. Atlanta. Both of us adjusting to a city. Parks and streets. Creating a home. Paint and plaster and makeshift carpentry. The arrival of Annie. A new life. A better life. How wonderful it was. Complete. Us watching the world unfold through new eyes. Then Mitt, life squared. And me. Me. Never telling Jill anything about the old me. About Abby.

Gray: "Every minute a secret stays a secret, it gets bigger. It develops a life of its own until it matures into a betrayal. Then it's too late. It ages with you. Five words – why didn't you tell me?"

Low voices. Gentle laughter, reeling me back into the moment. I untranced. There in the front seat, Abby and Jennifer. Like sisters. There out the window, strangely familiar territory.

Memory jolt. We were nearing the canyon. Abby's voice. Happy. Sunflowers.

"You've been awfully quiet."

"Just…just letting you catch up."

"For five hours?"

Five hours. This was record time for this reality. No, nearly a record. Whatever. It didn't matter. I had a plan and it might work. We might make it to Missouri.

I heard sunflowers again, with a hint of wary.

"This is the longest you've ever gone without a cigarette."

Here, now. An opportunity. I could turn loathsome me into a liar. I could tell Abby and Jennifer I quit. Then, when Loathsome Me lit up, well, they'd light him up. Then, no. Why confuse them?

"I dunno. Here in the car? It didn't seem right. You know, fair."

Abby almost drove off the highway trying to see my face in the mirror. Jennifer applauded.

I needed to change the subject. "We're nearing Flagstaff. We need a place to stay."

Abby eyed me in the mirror. "You've been to Flagstaff?"

Oops.

"I've seen maps."

A place to stay. Again, part of the plan with no plan.

Two rooms? One room? Who would expect to sleep where? The Dopp Kit, was it mine? Did the Loathsome Me occasionally overnight at Abby's? Were we an item? An odd item? Did Jennifer know this?

I saw Abby's eyes in the mirror searching mine. Then the jimjams. The cold creeps. Why? Because I still needed the firchose. Jill wouldn't understand that. She couldn't. I couldn't. Who could? Then it all fell apart. I wanted out, wanted to go home. Whatever this was, I didn't have the moxie to face it. I longed to see the black and white hand and its governing coin.

Then, no.

No.

Abby wheeled into a roadside tourist trap – gas, junk food, and a thousand impulse buys. They also had a rack of pull-card promotions for motels and restaurants and delights and diversions. I pulled card after card until I heard a squeaky chipmunk voice that carried the room. I replaced the cards. We didn't need a card. We had Betty.

The space Betty occupied could be measured in square feet. She was as wide as she was tall as she was deep. Four feet in each direction. Add a vertical foot for the cotton candy hair. But that's not what you noticed first.

First, you noticed her oversized glasses. Black and wide and pointy with the cartoon characters Krazy Kat and Ignatz Mouse perched on opposite ends like statues, anchored by an entirely unnecessary baubled chain around her neck. If the glasses fell, they would land flat on the ample moo-moo-draped deck of Betty's square footage.

There are two kinds of people who work tourist traps – those who love tourists and those who don't. Betty was a lover. She and Abby were fully engaged, with Betty delivering the lowdown on motels. It was the off-season.

There would be vacancies. She narrowed the choices to two.

Abby pressed her. "Which would you stay in?"

"Oh, honey, it's six of one, half a dozen of the other." She paused. Her eyes held mine. Her voice seemed to drag. "You could flip a coin."

Whatever it was I said or gurgled, it must have been loud, because it brought the room to a standstill. All eyes were on me. I caught myself in a security mirror. Fear.

Coverup time. I went with choking. I clutched my upper chest and began coughing and hacking. I bent over to rush blood to my face and waited for the smoky voice and the black and white hand and the coin.

Quick reconnoiter. No voice. No hand. No fifty-cent piece. No pins and needles. Betty wasn't going to flip me. I squeezed some tears and came back up. Deep exhale and a "whew," as I fanned my face.

Jennifer was there. She pounded my back. "You alright?"

I hacked out a yes and all eyes went away. Abby finished up and we left with a bag of genuine tourist trap doodads.

Travel creates a bond. It just does. Every event is beyond routine and lives in sharper focus. Even the ordinary is out of the ordinary. It imprints on you. You must adjust to your companions to make it work. I could feel the bond. It split me. It made me warm and queasy at the same time.

Jennifer rifled the bag of doodads, producing them one at a time while she and Abby did a running commentary in Betty's chipmunk voice. I found myself joining in.

A bond. The bond. And then the burden. All of it. The remorse, like being dragged underwater. Mitt, Annie, Jill. Why wasn't I laughing with them? What were they doing? Was the East Coast facsimile of me even with them?

Stop. What I was doing in this West Coast world was

something that needed to be done. I steadied myself to stay on mission.

I pushed back into my seat. Up front, Abby's face appeared in semi-profile. The angle washed away the years. It was 1964 again. Another whipsaw. Firehose. It would need to stay on.

***

I'd had so many moments of truth in my dual-world journeys, you'd think I would have grown accustomed to them. I hadn't, and here was another one. We were under the unmistakably kitschy carport of the Waputki Inn. Glass and steel at a pitched diagonal. It was about to be who-is-in-what-room time. I braced myself for the inescapable and started to open the door. Abby gave me my escape.

"You all just stay here."

Exhale. "You all." Sunflowers. We waited and watched Abby through the overlarge window.

The Waputki. Now I knew what Abby and Betty were chewing over back at the trap. This was absolute Abby. The tackiest motel within driving distance. Unchanged since 1950 all the way down to the "W" made out of arrowheads. New coats of paint over countless old ones preserved the white, sienna, pink, and aqua. I watched as Abby collected two sets of keys.

Two. Okay. First problem down.

Adjoining rooms. Pine paneling. The place was like a museum. No, it was a time capsule with a door and a key.

Whipsaw again. Every moment Jill and I spent on our Grand Canyon honeymoon cost more money than we had. This was the sweet part of the memory. Sweet and rich. Jill had watched as I broke a sweat planning nights of golden memories. We would stay at the elegant places and swagger into the cloth napkin joints. She braked me.

"Let's just be us."

She was so right, but I still wanted just one golden moment. One. On a chosen night, we dressed up and ambled into a fine restaurant, finer by a mile than anything either of us had ever tried. We laughed. We drank wine. We lived outside ourselves. Ask me anything about that night and I'll replay it for you by the second, all the way down to the feel of the tablecloth.

And now here we were. Abby, Jennifer, and I, this time me with a fat wallet, doing takeout from a hamburger stand. Make that the kitschiest hamburger stand in town. Whipsaw.

We closed the night playing Scrabble on the bed in the girls' room. Abby produced the game from somewhere. Rarely – okay, never – had Scrabble given me chills, but there they were, the words. My words, lined up on the little wooden tray as the game moved forward.

Home.

Family.

Time.

Kids.

Fate.

I didn't try to win the game.

Bedtime. I crossed into my room and heard the door lock click. Reassuring, then not assuring. My room closed in on me. It didn't help that the pink arrowhead lampshades rouged everything. Walls. Ceiling. Furniture. Drapes. The color blended with the dark and washed the warmth out of the red. Magenta hinting toward maroon. Somebody back in an era of two-toned cars must have thought this was romantic, even sexy. It wasn't, especially when viewed alone. You could almost hear a funeral organ.

It had been a full day in this world, and each additional minute set a record for duration. How would it end? The black and white hand and the smoky voice always came from nowhere.

Time to shake off the dread. I unplugged the television. I was alone in the room with nobody but me to transform into the Black and White Man. Time for a look at what Abby packed.

I didn't hate the clothes. Didn't like them, either. They just weren't me. The real me.

Pause. The real me?

For the first time in 16 years, I had to ask just who that was. Was the real me in Abby's bag and not what I saw in a mirror? Was Atlanta me the phony? What was I at my core? My core in this reality? I searched for a word.

Contemptible? No, that wasn't it. That didn't cover it.

Pacing, an activity that goes stale fast in a small room. I caught myself in the mirror. Well, half myself. Half my non-broken nose face appeared inside the frame, broiling in the non-red red. It was a face I didn't seem to know and didn't want to know.

The word came. Wicked.

Chills. Janus. I wiped my cheek with my hand. The red stayed.

Whipsaw. I needed Jill. Her foundation.

I needed the absolute sunlit faith in me that I saw in the eyes of my children. And I needed it bad.

Whipsaw. Children. Child. I've got one in the adjoining room. Or do I?

Whipsaw. Janus.

Reminder. Why was I doing this, all this? This trip? This

extended stay on this side of the coin?

The answer, of course, was Gray. All this, just for the chance to talk with him. He would have answers. He would understand the questions.

Understanding. Yes. That's what I needed. There was one place to get it.

I went to the phone and dialed Joel's pager. It picked up. I hung up and waited. The callback came right away. Too fast, really. I picked up.

It was an auto-message from a pest control company. In this world, Joel was a lacuna.

Exhale. Exhaustion.

Lights out, then sleep, without any understanding.

IX
DAY FOUR

New day, new mirror. The lifeless red hue was gone from the room. The face I shaved – the whole face – didn't seem malignant. It was just me with a nice nose. Me in a world I hadn't made.

This made sense in its own way. I was a traveler on this side of the coin, and here I was staying in a motel, like travelers do. It had to make sense, even just a little, for me to shake the qualms.

Morning. Normally, I would be delaying my departure from our Atlanta house, mousing around with two small children while a patient wife nudged me toward the door. Now, I was traveling, which inferred an eventual return to my own world. Or did it?

Whipsaw. I'd stayed overnight in this world because I needed an extended stay to see Gray. I didn't want it to be permanent.

Shake it off. Remember the goal. Splash some water and towel off the shaving cream. I turned and walked out of the bathroom.

"I wish you wouldn't wear those."

Well, this answered the boyfriend question.

Abby. Abby in my bed. I looked down at myself. I still had on the black silk boxers from the day before. Abby in my bed. She was a one-man woman and we were still an item.

One man. Me. My heart broke for her. What string of calamities and humiliations led her to accept this? A woman in the wings. A man spreading his. Black Lipstick Girl flashed before me. She seemed like a century ago.

Abby in my bed. Waiting. Her form beneath a sheet, and apparently nothing under that. Firehose. She spoke in a rushed murmur.

"I sent her for donuts. She's scouting for a lunch place. We have an hour."

Her. She. Jennifer. An hour.

Time. I had no idea what time it was. Morning. That I knew. The pine paneling color warmed with daylight even with the shades drawn.

Abby in my bed. Firehose. She shifted beneath the sheet. The room began to lose its warmth. Another murmur, less rushed.

"What is it?"

Where to start? The truth? I'd already decided against that. The truth wouldn't sound like the truth. How could it? My mouth was about to open. Whatever came it would have to do.

"I…I can't."

"Can't?"

I was still one step deep into the room. The adjoining room door was open. I stayed where I was.

"Please don't make me explain."

Abby sat up and pushed back against a pile of pillows. Abby. Pillows. You remember the small things. She liked pillows. She had brought pillows from her room. But this wasn't going to be

152

pillow talk. Her form shifted again. Holding the sheet up with her hands. Firehose.

"Oh, you're not getting off so easy. You've got some explaining to do."

I didn't move. Didn't speak. Her eyes swept me up and down, stopping to roll at my silk boxers.

"Somebody has gotten to you."

I thought of Jill.

"Oh, God. It's true."

Her arms went around her knees. She clutched them close. The sheet stayed up. Firehose.

"It's written all over you."

I made a ridiculous attempt to recompose my face. Into what, I'm not sure. She pressed me. "What are you doing? What are you doing to me? What have you done to yourself?"

Good question. Was I doing this to myself? There wasn't enough time to answer that one.

"It's like there are two of you."

How to say, "There are?"

"Who is she? How long? Where is she? What's her name? How did she...stop. No, don't. Just...I don't want to know. I don't want to know any of it."

She pulled her knees tighter. She was no longer looking at me. Me, in my ludicrous silk shorts.

"In these last days you've shown me the man I always knew you could...the man I've waited..."

She turned sideways, curled into a fetal position and pulled the sheet over her shoulders. No firehose.

"For God's sake, Matt."

Silence. Minutes, seconds, I don't know. She shot back up and leaned forward, her eyes drilling mine. "Is this some kind of game? Some kind of idiotic 'art' thing? You come to us and you are a different person. A better person. A fine person. For a few minutes, or an hour, you make us love you all over again. Then you go. Why are you torturing us?"

This deserved an answer. I started to speak, although I had no idea what would come out.

She raised her hand and stopped me. "No. No more Matt Andrews bullshit." She rarely swore. Almost never. Now, she spoke very slowly.

"How is it that the man I always knew was inside you…that man finally comes out and you give him to another woman?"

This time I raised my hand.

"Someone did get to me, but it wasn't a woman."

She gave me a raised eyebrow.

"And it was 16 years ago."

Her brow furrowed. Her eyes looked inward. I moved nearer the bed.

"The man was, is, the preacher we, I, am going to see. The preacher in Missouri."

I could see she knew I meant what I was saying. She softened.

"But, Matt. Sixteen years. Sixteen years of…why now? Why all of a sudden?"

Reason was not going to work here. Well, it could, but first we needed faith. I needed her faith in me.

"I've never told you I love you."

This surprised me, and then it didn't surprise me. It just came out. I wish I could describe the look she gave me. If I could, I would be a far better artist. It was like I had just infused her with sunlight and it beamed back out of her. There was a divinity to it. I saw her fingers go smooth as the tension released from her. I gave it a moment. Then, I had more.

"I do love you. I always have. I know I've put you through so much. Well, I don't know for sure, but I think I know. There isn't another woman, at least not in the way you think of it."

She looked confused. I understood.

"I love you, and right now I want you. I want to get in that bed with you, even in these loathsome shorts."

She smiled.

"But I can't."

Something replaced her smile. I couldn't tell you what it was. It was a look. A look too deep. Pain. No. An old agony, one she had become accustomed to, one she tried to wear on the inside. I had to fix it, or at least try, even though I knew I couldn't.

"I love you and I want you, but I don't want you in this way. It can't be this way. If only I could…I can't make you understand. I can't make anybody understand."

And then words failed me. It was nothing and everything. The never-ending spinning – Jill, Mitt, and Annie to Abby and Jennifer, and then back around. Atlanta, Los Angeles. Normal Me, Loathsome Me. Reality here, non-reality there. Longing, shame. Homesick there, embracing the road here. It was the weight, but it was the weight of nothing that felt like everything.

I didn't realize I was sitting on the end of the bed until I felt Abby's hand on my shoulder. I didn't realize I was crying until I looked up and felt tears on my cheeks. Her touch wasn't electric. No underground wires. She hugged me and I cried, but not like a baby.

A baby doesn't have that many years of regret.

But what did I regret? Did I regret what Loathsome Me put Abby through? And why? It never happened. Or did it? No, it couldn't. Anyway, that wasn't it. It was something else.

Something too deep for my own tears. The unbearable weight of nothing where there should be something.

And then it was scramble time. The sound of Abby's car pulling up outside the door. Abby was out of the sheets, nightgown in hand, and back in her room, pronto. I don't think her feet touched the ground. Firehose. The car door and the door between our rooms slammed shut at the same time. She forgot her pillows.

And why did this need to be hidden from Jennifer? Easy answer. Because Loathsome Me had managed to put shame in our marriage bed.

I dressed, the tears on my cheeks still wet.

✳✳✳

It's there in the name, The Grand Canyon. Actually, it's there in the "The." Other canyons don't get a "The." They're just canyons. And nobody has yet named a "Grander" Canyon.

I didn't allow myself to get caught up in the majesty of the Grand Canyon, which, of course, is not possible. Majesty is about all there is. But the Grand Canyon belonged to the past. To Jill and me. To us alone. We lost ourselves in the majesty on a storybook day so many years ago. I tried to keep myself in that moment.

This gave me some comfort. It was something real. Real and storybook at the same time. A connection to Jill. I could relax as much as you can relax while looking for answers in one world and wondering what is happening in another and all the while fearing a space-bending coin flip from nowhere.

Relax. I tried. I could. I could let the never-ending back

and forth between these two worlds rest for a bit. It was like the Grand Canyon was something I didn't owe Abby and Jennifer. No, owe is not right. I wanted to give it to Abby and Jennifer. I just didn't have to fully give them me along with it. Breathe.

Then Abby and Jennifer slipped their hands in mine. At the same time. How did they do that? They wanted all of me, and I felt myself giving it to them, giving in to the majesty, despite myself. I could feel myself passing through their hands.

Abby wanted still more. Our too-brief moment at the end of the bed wouldn't be enough for her. This I knew. I caught her eyeing me when she knew Jennifer wasn't looking. Turmoil, apprehension, love, all in one glance. I knew she wanted me to look at her the same way. The best I could do was throw her my don't-worry look. It wasn't enough. She wanted more and I didn't have a clue what to say.

Luckily, the Grand Canyon makes for a great distraction. I let it do the work.

I didn't allow myself to be impatient. I didn't hurry Abby and Jennifer, although I nixed the donkey ride, which I could tell actually relieved them. You can't hurry someone away from the Grand Canyon, but I was in a hurry.

Pressure. More and more I found myself surveying the crowd, looking over my shoulder for a colorless man who apparently only I could see.

Majesty and wait. Majesty and wait. I found myself looking at the ground just to escape the majesty, which only magnified the burden of the wait. How many hours? Too many hours until at last, we were back in the car.

I directed from the back seat as Abby backed out of the parking slot.

"We'll pick up Route 54 outside Albuquerque. Then

Missouri, here we come."

Abby braked and eyed me in the back seat. Before turning to steer out of the lot she gave me her hold-on-bub look.

"First, the Petrified Forest."

Jennifer squealed and clapped her hands. The Petrified Forest. Another "The." More majesty and wait. I was not in the mood. I'd seen enough for one day, but Jennifer was too pleased. I wouldn't deny her if I could. It was an hour down the road and it was on the way.

At least it would be my first time.

Jill and I didn't stop there on our trip. We passed through at the end of a day. The American Southwest had already filled our windshield for hours, so we just kept going.

Fine. This time, I would stop. I settled in.

As near as I could tell, the canyon did its work on Abby. It had erased the dicey morning moment for her, or at least made it dormant. She finally stopped giving me the eye. The eye. The last thing you want when you are carrying a secret, which I was, if you want to call it that.

Relieved of the eye, my thoughts turned to Jill, Mitt, and Annie. It would be naptime for Mitt and the house would be quiet. Jill would be using the time to go deep into her project for the day – she always had one. For Annie, dolls and plenty of them.

I had the usual mix of disquiet and serenity that came with these thoughts. I'd grown accustomed to the two-sided world, or worlds. Janus. Quantum Robin. Aching to be there. Having to be here.

We were about halfway to the Petrified Forest when it dawned on me that I, riding there in the back seat, had kept my eyes on Jennifer for too long. What was too long? I couldn't tell

158

you. I just knew it was too long.

I couldn't stop looking at her. She was so real and she seemed to be so much mine. Make that Abby's and mine.

The two in the front seat had forgotten me again. They were chatting. Happy. The painted desert was coming up and it would be right up Abby's alley.

Jennifer was just glad to be there. The thought of her hand in mine grew up inside my head. She was so alive. So truly alive. Alive and mine. I was pretty sure she'd never heard me say I love you.

✳✳✳

If time expands at the Grand Canyon, it stops in the Petrified Forest. For me, it stopped earlier when we passed the turn onto Route 666, A.K.A. "Satan's Highway." Let me tell you, the last thing a guy stuck between two worlds needs is a reminder of hogwash numerology, but there it was. Hogwash or not, it gave me chills. What if we turned? What if this meandering journey from nowhere to nowhere went somewhere? Somewhere marinated in evil. Well, it would be lonely. It was all lonely. Desert landscape. Everywhere. Chills.

I tried to escape the chills. Tried to slip into my warm pool of memories of Jill. Didn't work. Numerology. Hogwash. Journey to nowhere. Leave me alone.

And then we were there, or more precisely, we entered the zone. I was right about Abby. The painted desert was right up her alley. You could have tried to count the times she longed out loud for a canvas and easel, but you could only try. She dragged us from one breathless eyeful to another. I suffered through the thing, the scenery, not Abby. Scenic grandeur doesn't mean much when all you want is an answer. Scenery is all questions.

And then she let us go and skipped ahead of us. We watched her bouncing along, all joy, as she distanced herself. I felt Jennifer's hand slip into mine and the same electric mix. Joy and aching. Wanting to be there and wanting to be home. Home. Mitt and Annie.

Jennifer squeezed my hand. "Does this mean you're coming home?"

She spoke quietly, but she didn't need to. Abby was too far away. There was a searching in her voice. No, a longing. Or, maybe, a plea. We did not look at each other. We watched Abby – happy Abby – up ahead of us.

I knew I owed Jennifer something, but what? There was so much I didn't know. Was this the first time she'd ever asked me if I was coming home? Something inside me doubted it.

She didn't seem to be in a hurry for an answer. I turned to her. She looked up at me and I took in her face front on. All of it. It was the first time, really, that I'd regarded her that way. And I saw myself, at least for a moment. Her features seemed to shift and recompose themselves into different reflections. Abby to me to Abby to me to Abby to me. But there I was in her face.

It was so wrong, what was happening to her. I saw myself at age 16. My parents gave me all a child needs. Love. Respect. Support. My response? Anger. Dislocation.

But here, in this world, she was the opposite. I could see myself in her face but she was the opposite of me. I had given her nothing. At least, that's what I assumed. Maybe I'd been around more in her early years, but I would still have been a father in black silk boxers. I'd given her so little and she returned it with what? I searched her face. There it was. Love. And forgiveness and I was guessing there was plenty of that. It went inside me and I knew it would never leave.

I took both her hands and said exactly what I meant.

"I don't deserve you."

She laughed. This surprised me. Her response seemed, well, mature.

"That's what mom says about you all the time."

Of course she did. Abby always levels with you. But I needed Jennifer's opinion. "What do you think?"

"I think you're acting."

You ask a question. You never know where the answer will take you. I wanted to hear it. She didn't seem to be uneasy about saying it. She had Abby in her.

"Am I a good actor?"

"Good enough for most people, but not for mom and me. You're like some of the kids I see in school. You want people to think you are one kind of person, but really you are another kind. It goes both ways. Mostly it's people who are mean pretending to be nice. Sometimes it's people who are sensitive pretending to be tough and hard and everything. They act like they don't care about anything when they really care about everything."

"So, which am I?"

"Oh, dad, don't be silly."

Oh, dad. The words were magic. I squeezed her hands and I could feel her running through me and staying put. Exhale. Peace. But not enough peace. There was still a question in the air. I could only deliver honesty.

"I don't know if I'm coming home, Jennifer."

"You don't have to worry about mom, she wants you to."

"It's not that. It's…it's me."

"She wants you to a lot. I know. I know, well…" She glanced

up at me. "Mom forgot her pillows this morning."

Okay. Another mystery solved. Jennifer knew. But, to me anyway, that made things worse. What was it that added up to "us" for Abby and me? Time to go detective. I would ask Jennifer what I could not, would not, ask Abby. But how? Something told me she would see through the "act like I have amnesia" routine. Sometimes when you need an answer, you just aim the dart at the bullseye.

"Why does your mother stay with me?"

"Stay?"

"Put up with me. Not kick me to the curb. Why doesn't she just let go of me?"

"Oh, that's easy."

Easy. The last thing I expected. She had more.

"It's not that she won't let go of you. It's that you can't let go of her."

Like I said. You ask a question, you get an answer. I gave her my please-keep-going look.

"Just when she's had enough of you, that's when you do something that is irresistible for her. It's like you have a sixth sense. You just know it. You know the right time to bring her back to you and you know just how to do it."

This from the mouth of a sixteen-year-old. I looked at her and asked the only question I could.

"How do you know all this?"

"Because you do the same thing to me."

I think she saw the flash of agony that swept over me. I could feel her hasten to relieve the moment.

"But it's not exactly the same."

"How is it not the same?"

"You never let me get that far away from you. You never cut

me loose like you do mom."

I could feel that she was just warming up. It dawned on me that she'd wanted to say these things for some time.

"She always talks about you. She talks about you every day. Lately, she doesn't stop talking about you."

I gave her my keep-talking look.

"Mom says you are two people."

"You mean I'm like two people."

"No, she means two people. She says there's a whole 'nother person inside you. A better person."

This I knew. I heard it from her that morning while I was standing in my silk boxers, but Abby didn't tell me why she kept waiting on that good person. Now, I also understood that Abby and Jennifer talked almost like sisters, so my next question didn't seem too far out there for a sixteen-year-old.

"Why doesn't your mother see other men?"

"She says you're a force of nature. She says she feels it every time you walk into a room. She says it's very hard to find another force of nature."

Jennifer laughed on that one. Something told me that Abby laughed when she said it to her. Something also told me Abby's laugh sounded hollow.

"So, I'm a force of nature."

"Mom thinks everybody feels it."

"Do you think everybody feels it?"

"I think...I think sometimes you scare people."

Another sweep of agony. Another please-keep-going look.

"There are times you pretend to be too tough. There are..."

I stopped her with a look. It wasn't intentional. I just didn't want to hear more on that topic. There was too much Nebraska in it. I knew where it was going and I could feel it closing in on me. I changed the subject.

"Do you think I'm two people?"

Jennifer stopped being sixteen. It was a fleeting moment, but you could feel it.

"Yes…well, yes lately, the last few days."

There it was again. I needed to tell the truth, but the truth would only create disarray. Time to let her off the hook. I took both her hands.

"Jennifer, I know I've been confusing you lately."

Her youthful sparkle returned. Sixteen again.

"I'm not confused. You're just not acting." She squeezed my hands. "The real, nice you is there. You're here right now."

It came from within me, unbidden, the words I wasn't sure I had the right to say. "Jennifer, I love you."

She beamed and squeezed my hands again.

"Well, looky here, holding hands. What are we, making vows?" It was Abby, back from bouncing about the painted scenery.

Jennifer saved the day. Sunrise smile. "Dad says I can't drive unless you say so."

Jennifer's prevarication sold. Abby gave her one of those parent looks that say maybe but really means unlikely. And then we escaped.

We picked up Route 54 on the other side of Albuquerque. Heading north and east. We would go in and out of Texas twice, pass through Wichita, cross the Kansas line and head into central Missouri. Desert to prairie. There were other routes, but this one, Route 54, is the one Jill and I took. Retracing the trip made her seem part of it.

It got colder and grayer as the day progressed. Abby and Jennifer were up for a long drive. I'd given them the morning.

164

They gave me the rest of the day. We'd make it to Wichita. Nine hours.

Everything outside the windows reminded me of Jill. Everything inside the car was all Abby and Jennifer. The spinning continued. And then it was night. Neon. Vacancy. Hamburgers in one room, beds in separate rooms.

And then nothing. Emptiness. Me alone and horizontal with an unplugged television.

Morning would come on its own. There wouldn't be time for a replay of yesterday's encounter. Tomorrow would be coffee, donuts, red eyes, and another ten hours of road. Maybe.

X
DAY FIVE

Not all love songs are waltzes, but all waltzes are love songs, and there was one in the air, actually on the air.

Abby poked the car radio as the low swells of Kansas streamed along outside. You can't take Nebraska out of the girl. Country stations, just what I didn't need. The longer I stayed on this side of the coin, the more emotional U-turns came my way. Abby, Jennifer. Jill, Mitt, Annie. Throw in a lonesome country waltz and no heartstring goes un-tugged.

Escape. I didn't want to look at Abby while a soundtrack added an emotional layer. I couldn't endure a duet. Escape. Any escape. I turned to the window. It helped. Farmland is scenery. You either get that or you don't. You have to see beauty in things unromantic. Silos and fields can be fountains and gardens. Every farm tells a story if you know how to look, and the best time to look is on a drab, colorless winter day when you can see through the trees and tell what was done and undone at season's end.

Then there's the innate design. The human scale. The sensible organization. I'll bet if you measured the distance from house to barn on a hundred farms, they'd all be within 20 yards of each other.

You can't paint a winter country landscape without using black, and lots of it. It's under everything. Below the grays and lingering greens and browns and whites. Below the frost. Below the ice. Below the leaves and twigs and the water in the creek. It's the wet and chill. Shades on the bark on the trees. Deepening the shadows. I didn't like it. Black. Not the scene I wanted to paint, if I could paint.

As we drove north, the sky became the color of cold – flat and low and lifeless. I turned from the window. It had been an escape. It should have been longer.

Our route took us south of Kansas City. I had not returned since the morning I passed through it 16 years before. Anger. Frustration. Stupidity. Those I didn't need to relive, but I did. The warmth of Jill disappeared, and was replaced by me.

Me escaping that little Nebraska town. Me drunk on the road. Me not turning back. Me here in the back seat. Back where I was or would have been. Me in the mirror.

After I don't know how many hours the rolling prairie gave way to the Ozarks. Hills and lakes and sideshow billboards. A carnival in faded paint. Cartoon hillbilly characters with exclamation point promises that were out of season in the winter chill. Then it leveled off again. I was nearing home. My real home. The Black and White Man had let me get this far. Would he yank me just before the finish line?

We rode out of the hills and onto the southern lip of the great prairie that levels everything in its path all the way through Canada. I got a feeling of home that only familiar terrain can deliver.

Exhale. I felt like me for the first time in how long? Five days? A lifetime? It didn't seem to matter.

We stayed at a truck stop motel where Route 54 meets the interstate. I knew the place from my Missouri days, except it was bigger now, a lot bigger, and busier. Over the years it had grown into an asphalt lake, maybe 20 acres, with our motel at the most distant edge.

Outside, truck motors idling loud enough you had to yell. Inside, a pillow over your ears.

Two rooms. No adjoining door.

Late dinner at the diner, a neon, glass and steel island in the center of the asphalt lake. Too much to think about and too tired to fret. What was next, tomorrow, would take some explaining.

Abby would want to meet Gray. Of course she would, and of course she couldn't. I'd told her we were coming to see a man who had a great influence on my life. I was pretty sure when we met, Gray wouldn't know me. He needed to hear the full story. It was a story that would be impossible for her to understand, much less believe, so I'd be struggling to persuade two people.

No. I needed Gray's, and only Gray's, full attention. Absolutely no.

Tomorrow. We'll deal with it tomorrow.

What does tomorrow mean? Is it when the clock clicks past midnight? Or is it when you wake up to a new day? This is the kind of question you ask yourself when all you want to do is sleep and you can't.

My eyes shot open at 3 a.m. and they stayed open. Thoughts spinning in a loop. Gray. Tomorrow. Truth. Abby. Jennifer. Jill. Mitt. Annie. Heads. Tails. Please.

And on and on. Interrupted by idiocy. Images flashing. Mental photo albums. Me trying to remember traces of meaningless song lyrics. Me reshaping the sheets in vain. Me wondering if the Sphinx is a dog or a cat. Stupid things. Idiocy.

And fear, childish fear. A black and white hand. Maybe from under the bed. *Oh-for-God's-sake-Matt.*

And on, and on. Gray. Questions. Answers. Eyes toward the ceiling.

Until light washed the room.

XI
DAY SIX

Abby was steaming. Hot angry.

It was my fault. When she pinned me down outside the motel room with Jennifer alongside, I decided to go with the truth.

It went like this:

Abby: "So, we can't go with you."

Me: "Right."

Abby: "We drive all the way across the country to see a man you've never mentioned before who you say turned your life around and he's a preacher at a church near here and you're going to see him and talk about I don't know what and I, we, can't go with you."

Me: "Right."

Abby: "Fourteen, no, twenty, twenty-five hours in a car. I, we, both of us, deserve a reason. Why can't we see him?"

Me: "Because…because when we meet, he won't know me."

Abby: "Oh, for God's sake, Matt."

Me: "I know it's hard to digest."

Abby: "Digest? How, how can someone change your life if

171

you've never met him? Digest? Is he some kind of writer or guru? You never said anything about a book or anything. Digest."

Me: "The other morning, in the motel, you said you are seeing me finally as the man you always knew was there and it's good, or something pretty much like that."

Jennifer's eyes passed from Abby to me and back as she heard this, which made Abby glance at Jennifer and shift.

"Yes, something pretty much like that."

Me: "Well, can you take it from the new man that as strange as it seems, this is the truth and I need to do this alone?"

This stumped Abby. She folded her arms across her chest and gave me the stink eye. Jennifer was confused, but her eye was on the diner in the middle of the asphalt lake. Sixteen. Breakfast trumps everything.

I got in the car.

✳✳✳

It's peaceful, Missouri in winter. There's a goodness to it, especially when the hum and whoosh of the interstate is replaced by the crunch of gravel under your tires. You can hear birdsong even as you move. The birds to return in January. It gave me that home feeling again, which was about the only thing keeping me from chewing on my steering wheel. With the motel and Abby and Jennifer a few miles behind, my windshield gathered a colorless sky.

Just when you think you've got regrets to spare, another one piles on. Jill and I hadn't been here since Annie was an infant. We made the two-day drive to show off our firstborn. Then, life got in the way. We never had enough time for another trip. No, that wasn't it, and that was the regret. We never made time. Gray would get phone calls and notes. Jill's family would get those, too, plus way too many photos of the children.

Then, the regret vanished because it dawned on me it couldn't be a regret on this side of the coin, which gave me a wholly new and more potent kind of queasy. Today, on the gravel road I had driven so many times, Jill, Annie, and Mitt couldn't be there at all. It wasn't a matter of making time. They weren't in this time.

The queasiness faded as I made my way down the road. There was a strange comfort to that road for me. It led to the place where I once ended up on fire and grateful. The sense of comfort swelled as the long, familiar bend in the road that revealed Gray's church neared.

Over the years, every time I rounded that curve, I pictured myself in the cab of my truck, drunk and stupid in the night, about to be rescued in more ways than one.

This time I didn't know if I was grateful. In this life, I'd never driven this road, and now here it was. The familiar curve. I slowed and checked my mirror. Nothing approaching, so I stopped and looked right. Up ahead was the church, just as it should be. There was the old cemetery with the little fence. Chickens. Chickens roaming the cemetery. The house. The trees. I couldn't see behind the buildings where the little pond was, where the gazebo would be. Or should be. It was a colorless picture, but it felt warm to me nonetheless.

I was about to encounter some kind of truth. No, I was about to encounter the closest thing to the truth I would get. Whatever Gray said to me would be true. It would be real, even in this unreal world.

For the first time since I set out to see him, I was genuinely frightened. What if his truth and mine were different? Wait, of course they were. They had to be or I never lived my Atlanta life. My real life.

He had been the first person I wanted to see and the last person I wanted to see since Joel and I cooked up this encounter. Not seeing him required an act of will I didn't possess. Now it was either chew the wheel or hit the gas and turn in. I hit the gas. I needed Gray's magic. Again.

I turned in. Past the mailbox and over the culvert. I pulled into the church drive. You can't really tell where the dirt and gravel stop and the grass starts on a driveway like this. You just pick where to stop.

I watched my feet exit the car. Door slam. Crunch, crunch across the mix of gravel and grass. Tap, tap on paving stones. The door. Gray's little home and office. I knew he already knew a guest had arrived. You can't hide the sounds. It's too quiet out here. He would be coming to the door. He never waited for the knock.

And there he was. Gray Jarvis, all sixty years and six feet of him. Broad build. Traces of an athlete. Remnants of auburn in a swirling mantle that had never seen comb or brush. Squarish, reddish, blue-eyed mug behind rimless spectacles. Gentle.

Gray looked at me. Nothing. He looked again, and had a shock of recognition.

I answered it. "Please say that you know me."

"I…I do."

"You do."

Now things were better and they were worse. Good news and bad news tumbled and wrestled across my brain. What did that mean? He knows me in this reality? My second reality? Or was it my first? What world was I in now?

There had been no coin flip.

Then he made it worse. "But, I don't."

"You don't."

"I know of you and your great painting. Am I supposed to know you in another way?"

The wrestling and tumbling stopped.

"Yes." I looked him long and hard in the eye. "And no."

Gray was a perceptive man. You could see he understood this to be more than a passing moment. Whatever he had been doing, or had planned to do, he put away. You could see it on his face. I'd seen it before. My time was his now.

"Maybe you should come inside."

He stepped away from the door. I followed. Down the hall and right. And there it was, the familiar sunlit office. I entered the house under a colorless sky, but the office was sunlit. Blue sky was now outside the windows. It was odd, too odd, but I let it go.

Almost all was as it should be. Oak. Oak furniture. Oak shelving. Oak drawers and panels. The corner view. I scanned the windows. The sudden blue sky. There was the pond. But, no gazebo.

We sat, and I wasted no time. Whatever time I had with Gray would be precious. The black and white hand could show up at any moment and take the time away.

I told him the whole story. All of it, fast. He listened. Gray knew how to listen. He turned his chair so that he was parallel with the desk. He leaned back, creaked his chair and stared away, hands at his chest, fingertips wide and skyward, forming a little tent below his chin. A raised brow here, the fingertips parting and retouching there, and the occasional chair creak told me he was deeply involved. It was odd and familiar at the same time. It felt like a confession.

When I arrived at the present, I stopped. Silence, and plenty of it. Creak. The chair. He swiveled the chair around and faced the desk. He leaned forward, his elbows resting on the old school writing mat. I could see his baton by the mat. He began.

"So, you wrecked your truck here many years…"

"Sixteen."

"Sixteen years ago. I pulled you from the wreck, nursed your injuries, and you stayed on as a handyman for the next few years."

"Yes."

"And this turned your life around."

"You. You turned my life around. You made me confront the good and bad inside myself."

As soon as I said it, I knew he would disagree. Gray wasn't the type to see himself as a savior.

"Well, we'll talk about that later. And then one day, suddenly you are transported into another life. Another place."

"My old life. I mean, not my old life. The life I would have if I had not stayed here."

"You told me what's in this other life. It's the life you believe you are in right now, right?

"Right."

"You told me how this life works. Tell me how it feels."

"It feels, it feels mixed, but mostly uncomfortable. I want to be two places at one time. In this world I'm different. No, I'm not different, I'm supposed to be different. I have a different past. Done different things. It's not a good past. Well parts of it. Actually, just one part, is good. But I don't like this person. Nobody does, I think. Then, this coin gets flipped."

"Tell me more about the coin."

"It's not just any coin. I don't know. If it gets flipped right now, I'm suddenly back in my old life, I mean, the life I've had over the last sixteen years since I met you. I'm the me I want to be and I have the family I want and the life I want. The life you gave me."

Gray's eyebrows rose on that one, but he returned to business.

"Fifty-cent piece, right? Then if it gets flipped again?"

"Right. Fifty-cent. If it lands on tails, I'm back to the other life."

"When you are in this life, the one you call the other life, the life you are in now, do you change?"

"No. But yes. I'm the me I want but I have a past I don't want. And that's the problem."

"What's the problem?"

"I think I want the old past, too. I mean, not all of it. Not the bad parts."

My own words took me by surprise. Whatever I was about to say next would be, well, whatever I was about to say. Both Gray and I would hear it for the first time. I knew I was talking way too fast, but that's how fast it came.

"The bad parts. The loathsome me. No. He can't return. That me stopped here. Here with you and this church. He's gone. But he's not gone in this world. That's the bad part. But the rest. Abby. My daughter..."

I realized I was standing up now. I realized this because I froze in place. Eyes wide, staring at who knows what a thousand miles away. I had just called Jennifer my daughter. My. Mine. I don't know how long I stood there. My gaze tunneled back into the room. I looked at Gray to see he was giving me his keep-going look. I did.

"I am growing to love people I shouldn't. No, I should. Can't. No. People I'm not supposed to love but I am supposed to love."

177

"Your wife and child. You're not supposed to love them?"

"I'm not supposed to have two families."

Silence. Then Gray began talking, but more to himself.

"In the life that you are calling your real life, the life that you were living here with me, you never told me about Abby and why you left Nebraska, correct?"

"Yes. I mean, no, I never told you about Abby."

"Why not?"

"It, all of it, just seemed to be in the past."

"It?"

There was weight in the word, the way he said it. I knew what Gray was doing. He'd done it so many times before. He was making me move forward when I wanted to move sideways. This time, though, I didn't know how. It. It was lost on me.

"It. My life. Me. That's about it, or I guess that's what it is about."

He let it go, changing the subject. "Two families. Two lives. Two of you. One stayed here. One..."

During our time together, Gray had given me his I-can't-help-you look from time to time. It wasn't often, but it meant that whatever I was dealing with was, at least at that moment, beyond the reach of him or anyone else. Sometimes it was because I was bewildered and didn't know why. Sometimes it was because I couldn't figure out how to adjust a vacuum cleaner and had tossed the wrench. He gave me that look now.

"Son, I..."

"No, please. No. I know what you're about to say. I know you. You are Gray. This is your church. You are a widower. Your wife died when you were both young. You will never have another dance partner. That's what you said. You listen to baseball on the radio. Your left foot gets cold at night. You hate

Brussels sprouts. You study Greek and Latin and Hebrew. The Cardinals. You listen to the Cardinals. You have a garden. I built you a gazebo for it. Bell peppers. Beans. Anybody can grow tomatoes. That's what you said. You will always…"

Gray stopped me with his hand. His expression had shifted as one shock of recognition pinballed into the next. The dance partner hit deep. You could see it in his eyes. He spoke slowly.

"Slow down. Tell me about this Gazebo. What did it look like?"

I began describing the thing with my hands.

"Look like? You designed it. I built it to your design. From the drawings. You called it your Orison Bower. Eight sides, one entrance. Pride, lust, gluttony, greed, sloth, wrath and envy. These were written at the top of each side."

"The seven deadly sins."

"And grace. Grace over the entrance, the eighth side."

He pointed out the window at the gazebo-less garden.

"And this is in the garden."

"Yes. I mean no. Of course, it's not there. I can see that. It's not there because I, me, me in this life wasn't ever here to build it. Please. You've got to believe me. I'll go nuts…oh, Hell. Sorry. I'm already nuts. I was right here. Here. For years. You gave me a job. Church sexton, which really means janitor. You made me finish high school. You made me apply to college. You…you loved me and forgave me and so did the congregation. You…"

I slumped into a chair. I was repeating myself. Then I shot back up. I pointed to the bottom drawer beneath the oak shelving. "The plans. Your drawings. They were in that drawer."

I launched toward the drawer. Gray rose from his chair. You could tell he was about to stop me until he thought better of it. I dove to my knees and tugged the drawer halfway open. It didn't

179

want to come. It got sideways. I yanked again. I would have torn the front panel off, but I felt a touch on my shoulder. I calmed.

Gray's hand reached over my shoulder and slid the drawer above mine open. He pulled out a large piece of rolled-up paper and handed it to me. He returned to his chair. I followed and unrolled the paper on his desk. There it was, the gazebo. And the written words "Orison Bower." We stared at it like it was something exotic, even though both of us knew exactly what it was.

Gray spoke first. "I don't know what to say. This is extraordinary. If you're a magician, I don't know how you did it. My Orison Bower."

"Nothing up my sleeves, Gray. And you told me to call you Gray."

"So much of me wants to believe you, but I have to say this still doesn't prove you were ever here."

I slumped back into the chair and spoke to the floor, my voice little more than a whisper. "We built it together. You and I. You used the project to teach me about people. It was the entrance for confronting the seven sins and it was the exit from them. Everything we ever did together was a lesson for me. Except grace. You said I had to figure that out for myself."

Gray's eyes lit up on that one.

"Sounds like me."

I shot back up.

"I have proof. Proof."

Gray gave me his okay-I'll-wait look. I spoke even faster.

"The treasure. The buried treasure."

Gray lost his okay-I'll-wait look. He almost moaned.

"Son, please."

"No, wait. It's not like that. Just, just follow me here. When I

180

dug the first footer for the gazebo, we uncovered a tin box full of Confederate money."

I pointed through the window toward where the non-gazebo was.

"There. It was right here. You called it a gift. You did this sermon on hoarding false treasure."

Gray shrugged, but you could tell it got his attention.

"Sounds like me. Again."

"Oh, it was you. Let's go. You and me. Now. A shovel. We can go. A shovel We can dig..."

Gray stopped me with his hand again.

"Let's just stay in here for now."

I fell back into the chair opposite his desk. Exhale. He pushed back from the desk a bit and swiveled his chair. He was sideways to me again, leaning back, eyes to the ceiling. One hand went into the air. I reached over and picked up the baton by his desk mat and slipped it into his hand. He began to wave it in a circle and stopped. His eyes slid sideways toward mine.

"I knew you'd want it." I shrugged. We both smiled. It was the first smile since I came through the door, although his smile was rattled. He started to conduct.

"I've been asked to pray for rain many times..."

"But you never have."

Gray stopped conducting. He kept his eyes ceilingward.

"For the sake of time and my sanity, don't stop me if you've heard me say it before."

He began conducting again.

"Out here, we live with what most people call 'acts of God' every day. Drought or a late spring or rain at harvest time don't mean much in the city. The lettuce shows up in the store either way. But here, well, you ask the members of this church and they'll tell you that they live in an act of God. The grass withers. The flower fades. They know what stands. So, we don't entertain all that many arguments about the nature of God. God just is. And we are His stewards."

The baton paused for a moment, like it was thinking.

"And then, well, the acts of Man. You can't hide the acts of Man, of yourself, in a small place like this. If you don't mend your fences we all see it. Out here, the generations come and go. We watch. We get to know each other early. We can pretty much tell where you are headed before you figure it out for yourself. And if it's the wrong way, we watch for you to turn around. Some do. Some don't. But we, us, all of us, this church, me, we're always here to help. Now that might be God working through us, or it may just be us. I believe it's God. Either way, we learn how to help and why from this."

He glanced my way. Yes, I was paying attention. I'd heard it before, but I wanted to hear it again. He went on.

"A God that isn't all-knowing isn't God. But knowing isn't the same as making it all happen. There's plenty of room for you in that one. Take the beginning story. In Eden, the Garden was ended by a decision. A human made a decision, and it was the end of innocence and the beginning of what we think of as free will. We've been looking back at it since. When you are young, you make decisions. You do things, and you think they disappear behind you, fading to nothing in your rear-view mirror. Then you get older, and one day you round a bend and there it is, waiting for you. What do you do? Well, it can be the beginning of an opportunity to understand the meaning of grace."

He stopped conducting and gave me his do-you-want-the-whole-lecture look. I gave him my please-keep-going look. Grace. This is the part Gray left untaught back in the gazebo days. I wanted to hear it. I didn't want to figure it out for myself.

"Grace is when it begins. Forgiveness doesn't make history go away. What you did still happened. You'll round lots of bends and your old decisions will be there again and again and again because that's who you are and who you were."

"So, I'm going to be, am being, haunted."

"If you want to call it that. Your job is to include who you were with who you are. Then you can become who you really are and accept the gift of grace."

"I don't…I want to understand."

"Free will. There is more than one. More than one will. We tend to think of free will as action. What you do. But there is another one. Inaction. What you let happen. Confronting the truth about yourself means grasping both and understanding them as equals. That's where grace comes in. Grace doesn't make your past go away. It's like you are burdened with debt and somebody pays it off for you. You may be debt free, but you're still the guy who ran up the bill in the first place. Grace requires accepting who you were. Accepting that you live in a world you made. Then you can start building who you are in a world made by different hands, giving hands."

He swiveled the chair to the desk, and his eyes fell on me.

"Your past can seem like the biggest part of who you are. After all, it includes everything you did up to this minute. Understood improperly, or better to say confronted improperly, it can obscure the present, the future. I think that's where you are."

He rose and turned to the window. He wasn't looking at me, which I knew meant it was time to listen.

"There is no Hebrew word in the Old Testament that can be translated as meaning 'guilt' in a narrow sense. Oh, it appears in translations, but that's the limitation of language. In the Old Testament, the concept of guilt is broad. It includes the act of sinning, taking responsibility for the sin, and the divine act of punishment. Guilt understood this way isn't simply liability under the law. It's total alienation from God. Guilt is the punishment."

He turned and pointed the baton at me.

"But it also includes the divine act of atonement."

He waved the baton away.

"I don't know what this is. I know I feel a deep connection to you, a person I've known for an hour. I know that some time in your past you were given a new foundation. You wanted this foundation and you accepted it."

He looked away.

"Son, you don't understand that grace is full forgiveness, not a path that uses shame as punishment. So, I don't think your foundation was, or is, finished. I think it remains unfinished. You say it was me. I helped you build this foundation. Well, if it was me, you need a better builder. If you will pardon the metaphor, you've got more concrete to pour."

I could tell by the look on his face that he was troubled by the look on mine. It was dawning on me that my journey here was born of a juvenile yearning. I wanted somebody to hand me an answer. Instead, I was handed more work to do. Work that I thought I'd already done. Pour a foundation. With what?

"It was Peter who said love covers a multitude of sins."

This wasn't the first time I had thought Gray could hear me thinking. He had more. Of course he had more.

"Love. Young people today talk of 'unconditional' love. This is a profound misunderstanding. It's a disordering of what is significant. You can say you love things. You love your new

184

shoes. What happens when the shoes wear out? Love becomes loved. Here in this church, people aren't shoes. We only speak of one kind of love, and it's the kind you can use to pour a foundation, because it's the only kind there truly is. Here, love is not negotiated."

I'd been looking out the window, which often happened when Gray's musings transported me. My eyes returned when I heard the chair creak and looked up. He was seated again. He wore his time-for-a-new-subject look. He got this look when he knew I needed time to digest what he'd already given me.

He put the baton down.

"I have seen your great painting."

"You're changing the subject."

"I know."

"That's the second time you called it great. It's nothing."

"I have read about it, the many meanings. It's the mirror…"

"It is not the 'mirror of the Sistine Ceiling.' Please don't say that. It was my floor. The floor of my studio many years ago. I wasn't even there to paint it."

"The many layers. The many threads. The biblical numbers. The biblical dates. Moses. The Hebrew letters."

"They are just brushstrokes. I don't know. It doesn't mean anything. It's just junk on the floor."

"How do you know?"

"I don't. I don't know anything anymore. And now you. You are meant to be important to me. You were. You are."

"Let's stay on the painting. We can return to you and me later."

"There is no later. I could go any second. There is no time."

Gray picked up his baton. "Time. I'm glad you brought that up." He moved it in a slow circle, like a wand. "You say I taught you."

"Yes."

"Tell me, where is the first mention of time in the Bible?"

"Ecclesiastes. I don't remember the verse."

"Three, one."

"Oh, yeah, right. The beginning."

"What does it tell us, you?"

"That God made time for His use."

"His use. Not the use of a black and white hand."

"You don't understand. I could be flipped at any moment. I've been flipped by a television. You could flip me."

He gave me his take-this-to-the-bank look. "You are safe here."

Exhale. The familiar office. The familiar prairie on the other side of the window. The inexplicable blue sky. Safe. I knew it was true, although I couldn't tell you why. Yes, I could. Here, this place, was stronger than the black and white hand. Exhale again. I would go where Gray wanted to take me.

"Alright, my painting. My painting that isn't mine."

"I saw your painting in person after I read the many essays and monographs it has inspired. When I was told that you brought the term 'beresheet' to life, I had to see more than a photograph."

"Bear's head?"

"Well, that's how the word sounds. It's Hebrew for 'in the beginning.' After that, it depends on who you ask. For Jews, beresheet begins the first reading in the annual cycle of Torah study. Genesis 1:1 to 6:8. For Christians of a certain state of mind, beresheet has an entirely different meaning. It's called 'Jesus in Genesis 1:1.'"

I knew Gray was deliberately leading me away from

thoughts about myself, giving me room, so to speak. But you could tell by the way his baton was working that he really wanted us both to delve into this. He glanced my way. Yes, I was still paying attention.

"Here's the theory: the first sentence in the Bible contains a secret message about the crucifixion of Christ."

I'd heard this before, from Abby. But it just flowed in and out of my ears that day. I had the firehose on then. This was Gray. Gray Jarvis. Now, he really had my attention.

"Hebrew letters have individual meanings. Take the six letters that make up 'beresheet – beyt, resh, aleph, shin, yud, tav. Interpreted by the image associated with each letter, the meanings of the letters can form a sentence: 'The Son of God is destroyed by his own hand on the cross.'"

He paused to let this sink in. "That's the theory."

"You're telling me I brought this sentence to life."

"Yes."

"How? I don't even know what those Hebrew letters look like."

"You didn't use the letters. You used their pictograms."

I gave him my I-think-I-know-what-you-mean look. Joel's books. The ones I just thumbed through. Gray rose and went to the wall of drawers. He pulled out a rolled-up paper and flattened and anchored it on his desk. It was a large print of the painting. Then he pulled another sheet from the same drawer. I could tell by the title that it was the Hebrew alphabet. It was organized like a table. There were images and numbers by each letter.

"Remember, we are reading right to left. Tell me what you see when I point."

He moved his baton across the painting and stopped.

"A page from the Boy Scout manual. That's the thing about my floor. I was never a Boy…"

Gray arrested me with his hand. "It isn't what's on the floor. It's the images contained within them. It's not the bits of labels or advertisements or clippings and all the rest. Look inside them."

"A tent."

He pointed the baton to a package label.

"A man's head."

He lifted the baton. Another point.

"A bull's head."

Another.

"An ad for a dentist."

Gray gave me a look.

"Okay, teeth."

Another point.

"A hand."

One more.

"A pair of drumsticks, crossed."

Gray lifted his baton. "Those are the pictograms of beresheet – In The Beginning – the Hebrew letters you think you don't know."

He paused again to let this sink in. It did. Sort of. It would take a while.

"I get the crossed sticks as a cross and the hand. But a bull's head?"

"It's actually an ox's head. Here's how it translates. The ox's head is God. The tent and head translate as 'son.' Shin, the teeth, translate as consume or destroy. Son, God, destroy, hand, cross."

He didn't wait for this to sink in. He repointed his baton. "Now, read the numbers, right to left, on these parking tickets."

"Two, two, zero, zero, one, three, zero, zero, one, zero, four, zero, zero."

"Now, I'll break down these numbers for you. Two, two hundred, one, three hundred, ten, four hundred."

I shrugged.

"Hebrew letters and words are also numbers. It's called gematria, an alphanumeric code. In this way the Hebrew alphabet is similar to Greek. Those numbers – your numbers – translate to beyt, resh, aleph, shin, yud, tav. The letters of 'in the beginning.'"

Another baton point.

"Now read this road sign underneath it all. The one nailed to the floor."

"AA. It's a state highway sign."

"Aleph, aleph. One, one." He paused to let this sink in. "And what does the sign overlap?"

"It looks like a fraternity symbol. Greek letters."

He pulled the baton away. "It's alpha and omega. The beginning and the end. The first and the last. And what is this, partially covered by the Greek letters?"

I knew this. I knew this because Gray was a bird watcher.

"You taught me what it is. You watch birds at the feeder. There in the window behind your desk." I pointed.

Gray shrugged it off.. You could tell he wanted to stay on task. "Okay, so I taught you. What is it?"

"It's a goldfinch. Looks like it's painted on a postcard."

Gray brought his baton up. You could see he was moving into teaching mode.

"The goldfinch is a common symbol for Christian redemption in Renaissance painting. And what about your goldfinch?"

I leaned into the print and searched with my eyes. "It looks like he's, and it's a he, you can tell by the colors, it looks like he's in a cage. What's that got to do with beresheet?"

"Nothing. Then again, redemption in a cage. A painting in a painting. Any thoughts on what that could mean?"

Nothing from me. It was just another painting I didn't paint.

He looked away before he spoke to himself and me at the same time. "Perhaps there is more than one message on this canvas."

He returned to me, energized.

"There is much more. You've used tools, car parts, the lettering on beer cans and receipts, Monopoly Money, note cards, Scrabble pieces. You've included the pictographic interpretation of the Generations of Adam..."

He searched my eyes.

"...in their correct order. Adam, Seth, Enosh, Kenan, Mahalalel, Jared, Enoch, Methuselah, Lamech, Noah. And the order, step by step, points to..."

Another baton point. A return to the tent and head images.

"...the second Adam. Christ."

I stopped him with a look. "Gray, the connection seems vague."

He stopped me with a look. "What are the tent and head images covering?"

Any cartoonist could answer that one. It was Ben Franklin's 'Join or Die' cartoon, except only the dead carved-up snake was showing and the text was covered.

"After Eve, the first Adam succumbed to the temptation of the serpent. Christ, the second Adam, did not. Son, all of these, the pictograms, the numbers, the generations, all of these lead to the middle of the design. The middle where the alpha and omega and the goldfinch and the second Adam are. Now, look here."

I followed the baton. Bottom right above the first name on my signature.

"A watch. I never wore a watch."

"What time does it say?"

"Twelve twenty-five."

Gray put his baton down and picked up a Bible. He opened it, found a page and laid it in front of me. He pointed to Matthew 12:25. I read as he spoke.

"At that time Jesus said, "I praise you, Father, Lord of Heaven and Earth, because you have hidden these things from the wise and learned, and revealed them to little children."

He moved the Bible away. "Now have a look at this."

He pointed to a padlock, painted as though a little piece of cardboard was wired to it. On it was written what appeared to be the combination.

"What are the numbers here?"

I read them aloud. "Twenty, twenty-five, two."

Gray shuffled his Bible until he came to a page. "Proverbs is the twentieth book of the Bible. Chapter 25, Verse 2 reads, 'It is the glory of God to conceal a matter. But the glory of kings to search out a matter.'"

My eyes met his. His eyes never left mine.

"There are dozens more like this embedded in this painting. People are still discovering more. You really didn't know this before you painted it?"

I didn't answer. A thought was gluing itself into shape somewhere in the fog inside my head. And then a question. "What is twenty-three, sixty-nine, five?"

"I haven't seen that embedded in your painting."

"It's from somewhere else."

Gray shuffled his Bible again. "Psalms, Chapter 69, Verse 5.

'O God, You know my foolishness; And my sins are not hidden from You.'"

He watched me take this in.

Then he heard me breathe this out. "A presence that's really an absence. That's the statement."

I felt Gray's touch on my arm. "What is it, son?"

"It's the first thing I encountered when I was flipped. I was standing on it. It's complicated."

I knew Gray would try to understand this if I gave him context. I didn't give it to him. The moment was like a weight. I wanted to escape it, to toss it off, to put it away.

"It's…it's nothing. I don't think it is part of this. I don't know. I don't know."

I waved across the print of my painting that wasn't mine.

"This, all of it. This is just junk on my floor. How could I know?"

It was time for some kind of resolution, if there was going to be one. I leaned on the print and gave Gray my I-know-you-will-be-honest look. "I have a question for you."

It wasn't often I cross-examined Gray, but the moment required it. I knew he was versed in Greek and Hebrew and knew he was a deliberate thinker. He wouldn't be big on secret messages. I spoke slowly.

"Do you believe in the beresheet theory?"

He looked at me. "People are forever looking for evidence in science or history to 'prove' the stories in the Bible."

This was a Gray Jarvis preamble, and I never wanted to miss one of those. I knew a larger answer was coming.

I gave him my I'm-listening look.

"It comes up again and again. Someone claims to have discovered the remains of the Ark on a mountain top. Another wants to prove the Red Sea parted. Another says the Garden of Eden has been located. And on and on. And now this one, an embedded secret. A linguistic treasure map."

He picked up his baton. Arms spread. Big circle.

"What does any of that have to do with faith? Nothing. In this interpretation, it's the opposite of faith. It's grasping for validation."

The baton pointed back to the print. "Do I believe in this beresheet theory? No. At least I didn't until you and this painting came along. You made it a maybe. A very maybe, maybe."

I loved it when he said things like that. I gave him my please-continue look.

"Everything I know about Hebrew says the theory isn't plausible. Early Egyptian and Sumerian cultures used pictographic language, but even though Hebrew letters are associated with images, there's no evidence anyone used them that way. The letters don't stand for anything else other than numbers. Yes, there are images associated with letters, but it's a phonetic alphabet, like our own, like all alphabets with characters that number in the twenties. Tav is the 't' sound in the same way as tau in Greek or 't' in English."

He checked me again. I was still listening again. Baton again. Arms again. Circle again.

"It's also just common sense. How could twenty-two pictograms deliver any range of ideas? Pictographic languages need hundreds of image characters. They can have thousands. This also works in reverse. You could interpret the six symbols in Genesis 1:1 many different ways that would form equally logical sentence structures. And you have to combine two images to get the word 'son.' Why just those two? What happens if we combine others? You have to employ a ton of confirmation bias to pretzel

193

those six symbols into a single meaning. And finally, how could this have been a secret in plain sight for thousands of years? Beresheet is the opposite of faith. It's an expression of doubt. It's all too human."

He turned his attention from the alphabet to me. "And now you. You make it a maybe."

Another baton point. "I want to make one more stop on our tour of your painting. What is hand-written under your name on this court summons."

I had to bend over to look. The court summons was fill-in-the-blank. My name filled in the first blank. Then the typewritten words 'will appear' and then another blank.

"At one." It was painted as though it was written in pencil.

He watched me hard. I just stared back.

At one. Okay, at one. Nothing came to me. He made a circle with his baton to the space below the court summons. There was nothing there. A loosely formed black space.

He looked at me again. "What about this?"

"Nothing is there."

"I can see that. It is the only part of your 'floorscape' that is empty. What do you think it is?"

Again I whispered the words. "A place where something should be, and nothing is there. A presence that's really an absence."

You could see Gray taking his time absorbing this. "That's the second time you've said that."

"I know."

Gray swept his hand across the print. "These letters. Scrabble letters. See them scattered across the width of the painting. Small. Almost hidden. Far apart. What do you think?"

This meant he thought something already but wanted me to

get there. I read the letters. "E, N..."

"No. Read them backwards across the painting."

"A, I, S, C, H, U, N, E."

Gray watched me. I was clueless.

He filled me in. "It's pronounced 'ahee-skhoo-nay.' It's the English transliteration of the Greek word for shame."

The word sliced through me. Shame. I'd been bathing in it. I said it aloud. "Ahee-skhoo-nay."

"Why do you think it is here? Embedded backwards, and in Greek instead of Hebrew. Obvious enough in the context of many hidden things, but so out of place in the context of beresheet."

"I don't know. I don't want to know. It's just junk."

I turned away. I couldn't look at the painting anymore. No, I didn't want to look at it again, ever.

Gray's eyes caught mine. You could see him decide to drop it for now. He returned to the moment. "I read the interviews. You said over and over again that there was no underlying plan to this work. And you said it just now. That it was just 'junk on the floor.' If that is true, then this arrangement of symbols is the result of an influence that goes far beyond mere coincidence. And now I have you here, the only true source. And now I want you to look at me and answer. Did you arrange these images or is this truly how they came to appear on your floor?"

"I may be the source. I guess I am. But I have no idea."

Gray's face fell. I went on.

"Painters have signatures. It's called 'handling.' No matter how hard you try to hide your tracks, you leave clues. In poker, they call it a tell. If you look at enough paintings, you become conditioned to see them. I've looked at enough paintings."

I pointed toward the print.

"This isn't my hand. The first time the coin flipped me, I looked in my studio. Not my studio, I mean not the Atlanta me studio, but the West Coast me, the me I'm inhabiting now. The Atlanta me doesn't even have a studio. It's just a room. I'm a cartoonist with a table. In my West Coast studio, there was evidence of painting. Lots of it. The West Coast me had tried again and again to recreate this style but couldn't do it. The Atlanta me wouldn't have tried at all."

Gray's eyes stopped searching mine. He was persuaded. "If you didn't paint it, then who did?"

Instantly I knew the answer. I almost slapped myself, it was so obvious.

"Abby."

Gray's eyes started searching again.

"Abby? The mother of Jennifer?"

"Yes."

"The Abby and Jennifer who may or may not be our wife and daughter. The Abby who you say also saw this floor."

He looked away. He was quiet for a long time. Then he looked back and watched my face as he spoke. "Buried treasure."

"Buried treasure?"

"Just go with me on this."

He went back to the window, dropping the baton off at his desk on the way. He faced outward, hands behind his back.

"It has been many years since I was arrested mid-stride with the realization of just how small I am. There was no dramatic circumstance. It just dawned on me one day out there in the garden. But for a few friends and this congregation, and this restricted in time by a generation or two, what of me will be known? Well, that kind of thing keeps you thinking. Modern theory would have us believe we begin from nothing. As beings,

196

we were conceived of lightning and methane eons ago and wriggled forth, a membrane in a primordial soup. Time passes, lots of time, and we begin to organize ourselves into different, identifiable things. Dirt, rocks, tulips, dung beetles, bat colonies, sea bass, buzzards, badgers, yaks and plumbers, engineers and artists. Within this understanding you are defined as an 'it.' But what are you in the womb? What are you at the first gasp? Are you really an 'it?' At birth, do we enter a stream and flow with it, basking one moment and bouncing off rocks in another until we depart into a dead eddy? 'Put your hand in a bucket of water,' a friend says to me. 'Now, pull it out. When the ripples are gone, that is what remains of you.' But wait. Before we enter the stream, we are given a name. It changes everything. We are changed from an 'it' to a 'you.' A living thing goes from nothing to something with the simple application of a name. But what is this 'you' if it is emptied of any sense of divinity?"

He paused for a long time.

"Without a sense of divinity, this you is still an it. We can ask, 'Is that all? Is that where you stop?'"

I could tell he was waiting for me to speak. I didn't. I could've answered, except I couldn't. My mind was working too slowly. Sleepless. Overwhelmed. I didn't know what to say. He did.

"Or does a living thing start as a 'you' to become something else?"

Gray looked out the window for I don't know how long. Then he answered his own question.

"To become a thou."

He gave me time to let that sink in. It did, sort of. He went on.

"You cannot be or see a thou through reason. However far

197

we dig, we will never build a foundation based on reason. 'Thou' is past all categories of definition. To see a 'thou' in a 'you' is to make an ordinary person transcendent. It is to fill the emptiness with divinity. To see a 'thou' is to unearth a treasure that can't be seen. Within each of us is this treasure."

He turned back to me.

"That, my young friend, is a sermon I delivered on buried treasure."

I rose. "So, you did find the box."

"No. I didn't. The sermon was in response to another moment. Another issue. One we will, we must, return to. But first, you have more concrete to pour."

"You're telling me I'm looking for reason where none can be. A false treasure."

He retrieved his baton and came my way. We stood face to face.

"Far from it. I think your story is real. Very real. But I don't think it's happening here."

The baton pointed toward my forehead.

"I think it's happening here."

The baton touched my chest.

"I didn't turn your life around. You are turning as we speak. These people in your new life, the life you don't know is real, have become real. They went from an it to a you to a thou. You must confront this. You are asking me for a miracle. You are asking me to translate the illogic of your moment into something reasonable. You are asking me to pray for rain. You need to be looking for buried treasure."

He touched my chest again. "God does not despise a contrite heart. The miracle is here. 'At one' is a message to you. Think about it. You must translate it. You. Only you. But there is help.

198

You could start with the Book of James. In chapter 1, verse 24, he observes that you can see yourself in a mirror and then walk away and immediately forget what kind of man you saw. You said I made you confront the good and bad inside yourself. Did I?"

This I didn't need. A mirror. Me with a straight nose in a motel mirror. Red. Unremovable red. Wicked. Chills. It was too much.

I like to flatter myself with the idea that I have a quick mind. The Normal Me, anyway. Today it felt more like quicksand. Gray's words just disappeared into a maw. You could tell he knew this.

He put the baton away. I knew from many long talks with Gray that he would say no more. It was time for me to think. He put his hand on my shoulder and guided me ever so gently toward the door, down the hall, and outside into a sunless, colorless sky. The blue was gone if it was ever there.

He followed me to the end of the walk and looked like he was about to hug me. I shook his hand.

He pointed to the car. "We'll talk again tomorrow."

"There probably won't be one. I'll get flipped and call you from Atlanta tomorrow and you'll never know this happened. You'll only think you know who I am."

"I know that who you are is a great gift to the world."

"One single painting."

"That has charged the imaginations of countless people and maybe, just maybe, led them toward a better place. Remember, if you go away, as you say you might, so does the painting. At least, that's how I understand what you've told me."

I'd never considered this. No me, no painting. Did I care? Not really. I turned away. Once again the crunch, crunch on gravel and grass. Then, no. No. One thing more. I had to have it.

I returned to Gray. "I need you to do something."

"What is it?"

"I want you to flip a coin."

"Certainly."

This took me aback. He was so casual. Nonchalant. I took out my fifty-cent piece. "I mean this coin. And I want you to pray that I go where I am supposed to be and stay there."

The nonchalance faded. "Oh, son."

"Please."

"That's just magic with a prayer attached to it."

"Please."

"It doesn't work that way. I've never…"

"Prayed for rain, I know. Just this once. I'm begging you."

I put the coin in his palm. He considered it, holding it up like a jewel. "Okay, I'll flip the coin. You say the prayer."

"Okay."

He flipped. I closed my eyes while the coin was in the air. I prayed for an end to the madness. When I heard the coin hit his palm, I opened my eyes.

"Now, do you know me?"

I already knew the answer. There was no fade to black. No electric rush.

"Yes, son. I do. You are the same tortured man who was begging me to flip that coin a moment ago. Only now, you are more confused than ever."

Gray angered me countless times during our years together. That's what a good teacher does, really. Each time ended with me understanding I was angry with myself.

This time was different.

I couldn't control it. The old stubborn. The old stubborn just beneath the line to anger. The Nebraska me anger. It moved fast and found its way into muscle, bone and cell. It took over, just like in those very old days. I turned away from him, cold, and got in the car. Drove off too fast, spewing a little juvenile gravel. I almost made it to the mailbox.

The mailbox. The mailbox right next to the spot where the ditch meets the driveway. The culvert. The spot that stopped me here 16 years ago. The stubborn, the angry subsided. I braked. Exhale. Reverse. I eased the car back until Gray was beside my window. I rolled it down, looked him in the eye, and spoke. "I love you."

"You are loved, too, son."

He bent down, a question on his lips. "We agree that God made time for his own use?"

"Yes."

"Is there any mention in Scripture of God changing the past, changing history?"

"No."

"Is there any mention in Scripture of God deceiving people?"

"Yes."

"Remember those three answers."

He touched my shoulder. You could tell he had one more thing to say. You could tell he didn't want to say it. He said it.

"Jill, the woman you married, here in the gazebo." He said the word gazebo without a trace of irony. "What was her maiden name?"

"Nason."

Gray eased back from the window.

I put two and two together. "She still lives here, doesn't she?"

"If your story is correct, you'll remember where."

"Is she married?"

"No."

That was all he was going to give me. He leaned to the window again. You could see he didn't want to release me, even though we'd exhausted the moment. There was one more thing to say.

"You seem sure that you will be returned to your other state, 'flipped' as you say.

I nodded a yes.

"A question awaits you when your return to your other state, what you call the other side of the coin."

I could tell he was about to say something he didn't want to say but needed saying.

"A question for you only. It, the baby, Jennifer, what was her sacrifice?"

I could feel the question take lodging somewhere inside me. He didn't give me time to answer. His tone changed.

"What are your circumstances? Can I expect you tomorrow?"

My circumstances. Now there was a question. My circumstances. Hope and dread on two ends of a seesaw. Now what?

"What is there left to say?"

"I want to meet Abby. The Abby who made the painting."

Abby. One choice. Go back to the motel and the asphalt lake. Bring Abby back here. Another choice. Go to see Jill.

Jill. Jill and Abby only a few miles apart. It was a choice that wasn't a choice. For these last few days I had feared being flipped before I got to see Gray. Now what did I want?

What must I confront?

Jennifer. It to you to thou.

Abby. Abby and the painting.

Sacrifice.

The truth. Jill. Jill and…and what? So many questions, beginning with why, more than one why.

Exhale again. I gave Gray my hope-so look and drove away. I rounded the bend and the church disappeared in my mirror while countless questions arose in my head.

What was Jill like? Why was she unmarried? What would happen if I just came to see Jill? She certainly wasn't anticipating me.

Abby. The painting. Why was my name on the painting? Why did Abby do it? Did she do it? Of course she did. Did I force her? No, she couldn't be coerced like that. Then, why? Why? It couldn't have been a secret to me. It would take a studio to work in. A big one. And months to complete.

Jill, what was she like?

Abby.

Jill.

So close.

I found myself steering in Jill's direction. The direction I knew her family farm to be. Couldn't help it, really. It wasn't that far, but as I neared, a sense of unease grew within me. What did I think I was doing? What would seeing her do to me? To confront a version of her that was never in this West Coast life? Thoroughly, completely absent.

I crossed a small bridge and could see her house. There it was, as I knew it. On a rise. Barn. Chicken house. Outbuildings. I sensed the warm anticipation that always came over me as I neared being with her.

And then I went chill. In the distance, a young woman steered a tractor pulling a flatbed wagon through a gate near the barn. She stopped, closed the gate and headed toward the road.

She turned my way.

The warmth was gone. The idea of her driving past me, with us looking at each other, strangers, maybe doing the meaningless country wave, filled me with an emptiness beyond description.

I fired up Abby's car, reversed and hustled out a three-point turn. I disappeared from Jill's view as her tractor neared the bridge.

I drove fast. Too fast. It was an escape. Then, nothing in my rear-view mirror. No tractor. No Jill.

Exhale. I retraced the miles.

I neared an oh, so familiar turn. A right and I'd be heading to the interstate and Abby. A left and I'd be heading back to Gray. For a moment I considered turning back. Back to Jill. No again. I didn't want to see Jill anywhere but in my real home. What would seeing her in this world accomplish other than torture me? And it would be torture. To see the absence of recognition in her eyes. To see nothing where something should be.

I turned right. The interstate. No detour.

A noise guided my eyes in every direction. I braked. Jumpy. I was jumpy. I'd run over something. I got out and there in the road was a detour sign, rusty and disused. Ancient, if you can call a metal road sign ancient. The parallel didn't escape me. Think the word detour. See a detour sign. In a normal world it would be a coincidence. A creepy coincidence. In this world, it was just another sign, no pun intended.

I picked it up and leaned it against a nearby fence. I scanned the surrounding prairie. It was wide open and closing in on me. I'd grown accustomed to the feeling that I was being followed. The Black and White Man. He had to be following me. He had to know where I was.

That feeling had gone while I was with Gray. "You are safe

here."

Now, it returned. No, it was something else. I was being pursued. The perception of being trailed is one thing. Being overtaken is something else.

Tingles up the spine, like when you get to the door and sense somebody approaches behind you even though you know nobody is there.

Empty.

Fields and pastures muted under a pallid sky.

Silent.

Even the birds were gone.

Empty, but I kept looking over my shoulder anyway.

I got back in the car. A gleam of sunset cut through the gray ceiling. Squint. I yanked down my visor, and something fell out.

I watched. Slow-motion.

A coin. Black and white, slowly going end over end until it landed in my lap.

I heard a raw smoky chuckle.

Heads.

XII
DAY SEVEN

Joel. Joel from the morgue. Bedhead hair. Bulging eyes behind Coke-bottle glasses. Watching me like I was a science experiment as the now too familiar electric thrill and thump and swell of a thousand murmurs passed. I felt myself complete the return to myself.

Office. I was in my office. Of course, where else would Joel be? Joel in the chair, the one I kept for visitors. Me standing. Joel with a folder in his hand. Joel with a question.

"You just came back, didn't you?"

I gave him the only answer I could.

"I want to see my family."

I headed for the door. Joel arrested me. He whispered, urgent.

"Okay. But don't talk to Farley."

He handed me a folder.

"Take this. And don't you want your coat?"

I slowed.

"Yes and yes. I just came back and I want my coat. Is it still morning? Don't answer. I know it's morning."

I hit my door. Stopped and turned to Joel.

"I paged you. You weren't there."

"I wasn't where? Here?"

"The page went to somebody else, and yes, I dialed the right number."

"So, I'm not here if you're not here."

"I don't think that's it. I don't know. I only know your pager wasn't attached to you, or whatever."

"This is scary."

That meant something coming from Joel.

Time to reassure him. "I don't know what anything means, Joel, but it seems we're connected. Somehow. And, well, that seems good."

He gave me his look that said he would get around to understanding this. With that, I was gone. I had one arm in a coat sleeve and the folder in my other hand as I neared the elevator.

Farley emerged from his office. "Andrews, I need to see you."

I pushed past him and got to the elevator and smacked the down button.

Farley held up the papers in his hand. "Andrews. Now."

The elevator door opened. I stepped in.

His head. Magenta again. I didn't care. The doors closed.

Home, I wanted to be home. Jill, Mitt, Annie. The elevator crawled.

Elevator. Scene of my last flip. The anxiety grew as it stopped at each floor. In and out. In and out.

Nobody in a hurry but me. A vertical prison.

It was the same with the parking lot gate, the street traffic, and each and every traffic light between downtown and my house, except now the prison was horizontal. No amount of wheel pounding or teeth gnashing would speed up the plodding world around me.

Until my street. My block. My house. My drive. My walk. My door. My threshold. And…normal.

Everything was normal except me. Me with heavy breathing in the foyer. Annie making her I'm-with-my-dolls humming sound. Mitt gurgling in the kitchen. Jill coming out of the kitchen and down the hall, trying to dry her hands on her blouse. Mitt on her shoulder, baby bottle hanging, the nipple clenched between his teeth.

"You must have made deadline early."

Deadline. Work. Did I even draw a cartoon today? Did I care? No.

I took Jill and Mitt into my arms and embraced them. Long. Mitt struggled. I took him from Jill and put him on the floor. You could tell he wanted to be there. Then I laid an engagement night kiss on Jill. A long one. Very long. I poured myself into her. She came away, gobsmacked, and caught her breath.

And then I drank it all back in. My life. My wife. Mitt. Annie. Our house. Everything. It all felt new again.

For the rest of that day, I found my fingers tracing the textures of my life. My home. Our home. The woodwork. Picture frames. Fabrics. Dishes and cups and spoons. The pieces of my life looked new again. Shiny. Focused. Sharp. Every sound was comforting. I drank in more and drank and drank. If I wasn't holding Mitt, I was stroking Annie's hair or touching her hands or going side by side with Jill.

Routine. I wanted routine. All the normal you can serve, and then some. And that's what I got.

"Let's go out." This from Jill. "We haven't left the house in a week."

209

I would obey and happily so. She wasn't quick to voice her desires, so I knew she really wanted to go out. The snow. The kids. Cabin fever. We went out.

✳✳✳

How big does your world want to be? Four feet by four feet will do it. That was more or less the size of our table. One Andrews per side. Us looking at us. The rest of the world was around us, behind us, dropping sounds and dangling words we didn't care about. It was all there and it wasn't there. We faced inwards, an island in the rattle, clink and murmur.

How much love and contentment can a few square feet hold? There is no answer. You just keep pouring it in and you never stop because it never seems to be too full. You don't have to say anything. You can just sit there and look at each other. I don't recall what we ordered or ate. I could have sat there forever.

And then the sign came. The sign that all parents know. Mitt rubbed his eyes. The window on his day was closing. We settled up the bill and caravanned to the car.

After the kids were in bed, Jill and I headed down the stairs for the living room. It would be the usual. Couch. Wine. Me sitting. She prone. Me rubbing her feet.

Time for some detective work. I'd been gone for, what, three days? I had to know.

I started with an apology. "I'm sorry if I've seemed distant these last few days."

Antennae all the way up. The tone. The tone of her answer would be the answer.

"Usually you let go. You don't bring work home with you."

The tone. Not a hint of worry. Not a hint of anything. Just

Jill.

Whatever I'd been, the replacement me had been at least acceptable. I should have known. If she really had something on her mind she would have told me hours ago. Jill wasn't the type to let things smolder. I felt stupid. I wanted to reassure her.

"Won't happen again."

This was true. At least I wanted it to be true. I knew, or at least thought I knew, that I had controlled the last flip. Well, I didn't control the flip, but I had control over the duration of the stay. Maybe. No. Yes. I did have control. Otherwise, it was too much of a coincidence. I wanted to see Gray and I did. What I wanted to happen happened.

I dropped the detective mode. She was content. I was content.

I decided this would be the night that I would tell her about The Letter, which had turned into The Contract. It would be happy news. We would talk about signing it. We would talk about the future.

The future. Us. The kids. The world as an open map. Close your eyes and put your finger anywhere, and we could live there. We would talk, like during our drive to the Grand Canyon.

But, we didn't. I never mentioned The Contract. I didn't need the future right then. I needed now. I needed Jill. The future was next, anyway, so let it all come up later.

Movie time. Our little box of a television was the first we ever had with a remote control. When Jill reached for it, I stayed her hand with a touch of my fingers.

I gave her my let's-talk look. She gave me her what's-up look. I gave her my you-first look.

She quizzed with her eyes before she spoke. "What's on your mind?"

"When you first met me, who did you think I was?"

Another eye quiz. No answer from me.

"It's more like what were you."

I gave her my explain-that-one look. She held out her wine glass and gave me her pour-me-some look. I did, A sip before she spoke.

"You were so exotic. You showed up out of nowhere with hair like the boys in movies. You never spoke. You never smiled. Gray Jarvis told us you were special."

Special. This was news to me. She wasn't through.

"And then, with time you began to change. It was ever so slowly. You became approachable, sort of, but still mysterious. I thought you were so good looking, even with your nose. I started volunteering for things at the church because I knew you'd be there. That's where I saw you smile the first time."

The nose comment made me blush a bit. I gestured for her to keep going.

"Then, when you left for those years, I knew I missed you." She paused and looked at her hands. "More than you could know."

Her eyes turned upward and away.

"That's when I asked Gray about you."

Another newsflash.

"He said you were trying to leave one person behind so you could become a different person. When I asked him what kind of person you had been, he said he barely knew. He said you never talked of it, and he thought you might never talk of it. He said whatever it was, was too deep to know, maybe even for you."

Another newsflash. This one I knew I'd need to chew on for a while, but not now.

"Why didn't you ever ask me, you know, about those years?"

"I like what's in front me right now. What would knowing more change? Anyway, you'll tell me someday, when you're ready."

"Who…what do you think I am today?"

Her eyes turned to mine. "Matt, I believe in you. I've always believed in you. I didn't need Gray to tell me you are special."

She shifted, but our eyes stayed locked.

"Part of you is locked away. Sometimes I think Gray was right. It's even locked away from you."

Gray: "When you came here you didn't understand how to receive love. You didn't know what to do with it. You didn't know where to put it. In so many ways, you still don't, but the day will come that you do. It must come and it will come on its own. You can't bid it."

Her hand slid over and touched mine. "Someday you will let me in. All the way. I know it. When you do, we will be a better us."

"I thought we were a better us."

"Matt, there's always a better better."

"Better better?"

"How many times have I watched you wad up a drawing and throw it away so you can start over?"

That would be too many to count.

"Matt, that's what makes you better. It's one of the reasons I believe in you. You put yourself into your drawings. That's what sets you above the others. It is why people are drawn to your drawings."

She let out a little chortle. "Drawn to drawings."

I tried to find a smile. I couldn't.

Jill noticed and put her down-do-business face back on. "People see themselves in your drawings because you put yourself into your drawings."

She squeezed my hand and gave me a wifely look that was almost motherly.

"Someday you will put yourself into us like you do your art. All of you. We'll be better better." She looked upward and gripped my hand like it was too precious. "Better better better better."

There was nothing to say because I didn't know what to say. The woman I thought I knew had just revealed to me a depth of rare measure. She'd just drawn a picture of me that I couldn't wad up and throw away. I needed more.

"Why didn't you tell me this before?"

She squeezed my hand again. You could see she was using the moment to gather her thoughts. "I guess the easy answer is that you never asked me, because, well, you never asked me, but that's not it, really."

She looked upward again. "That day I asked Gray about you and he said he didn't know your past, he also said that I could know your future, that I already did know your future. He wasn't saying I could magically predict what you would do next. He was saying I knew what direction you were heading. He was right."

She returned her eyes to mine.

"Matt, every day you fulfill a promise for me. That direction I saw in you those years ago, you're still heading there. We're still heading there. I know you will never turn away, never turn back."

One more hand squeeze.

"I have only one wish. A few acres of farmland…"

We finished the sentence together. "…enough to need a barn."

Her wish was no secret. I knew she needed something to work on, something to manage other than me. It was my wish, too.

I switched the topic. "Do you ever think of our trip to the Grand Canyon?"

"Every day."

"Me, too."

She released my hand and lifted her wine glass. "It's funny. Now that we can afford a restaurant like that, I don't care if we ever go in one again."

I found a smile. She was already there. I had one more thing. "You know I love you."

"Of course. I know it every time you rub my feet. That's how you say it. Love."

She retrieved the remote, poked it and a movie flickered to life as she got horizontal and presented her feet to my lap. We watched another movie I'll never recall. No, she watched the movie. I watched her. I watched her imperfect features rearrange themselves into perfection. I let her flood into me and there it was. My own movie playing in my head. The day I saw her for the first time. The day I saw her again for the first time. The day I knew her presence made my day full. The day I knew her absence left me empty. The day I touched her and the sensation lingered long after I drew my hand away. The day that became the first time I ever knew what I truly wanted. The day Gray handed me her ring as she looked into my eyes and not at her own hand. And the days that followed. Jill, behind me when I knew I needed her there. Jill ahead of me when she knew I needed her there. Annie. Mitt.

Someday you will put yourself into us like you do your art. It wasn't a complaint. It was a guarantee.

Gray: "People say you have to work at a marriage. Fine, but it's not heavy lifting. Just keep her at the center. No day goes by in which you take her for granted. You'll be fine."

I'd never taken Jill for granted. I knew I never would. But I also knew that right at that moment I didn't know where the center was. No, I didn't know if there was a center.

When the movie was over, Jill was asleep on the couch. I more or less carried her to bed and laid down beside her. My foot touched hers. No words can describe how happy I was knowing she was there.

Tomorrow. I would tell her about The Contract tomorrow. Yes, I would sign it, and maybe she would get her barn. I closed my eyes.

And I opened them.

You've got more concrete to pour.

The dark closed in. Sleepless, restless dark. Minutes. Twenty minutes. An hour. Hour after hour after hour.

The trapdoor again. The brain door that wants to be unbolted and pushed open and won't be held down. The door that always wins and there's a gap. White noise. Louder. You push back. It almost closes. Again and again. Back and forth.

A question awaits you.

I tried laying on one side, pillow over me. I could hear and feel my own pulse washing in my ear. Relentless. Too fast. Too loud. Switch sides. Same thing. Another ear. No escape.

I found myself trapped in a mental loop. I pictured my hands trying to draw a form, a form that refused to take shape until I erased it and started over. Again and again and again.

Absence and presence.

Jill, Mitt, and Annie.

Abby and Jennifer.

Normal Me. Loathsome Me.

Longing and shame.

216

A question awaits you.

Whipsaw. Janus. Time, duality, beginnings and endings. Whipsaw. Abby. Firehose.

Jill. Jill right there beside me. "I believe in you."

I don't care who you are, you've got to have sleep. People will tell you they don't need sleep. It isn't true. Lack of sleep makes you stupid at best, crazy at worst. You're there and you aren't there at the same time.

I was somewhere beyond stupid, hoping I wasn't heading into crazy, lying in my bed, staring at the ceiling. Our ceiling. Jill and Me.

Ours, alone.

And not alone. The sensation of being pursued that emerged in Missouri on the other side of the coin never went away. It just got tamped down while I was with Jill and the kids. Now it returned, merciless.

A question awaits you.

I sensed another person in the room, someone watching and waiting. It wasn't altogether dark. I could see, but I couldn't see.

I got up and went to the closet. Tripped the light, enough to see but not enough to wake up Jill. Nothing. Nobody watching. No Black and White Man in the dark.

I almost laughed. Back to bed. Embarrassed, but not embarrassed. Pursued.

It had been 30 hours since I awoke to a darkened motel ceiling in Missouri. Impersonal by design. Trucks grumbling outside. Abby and Jennifer next door. Gray down the road, not knowing I was coming. I hadn't slept since that moment of awakening. I had barely slept all week. I didn't see any sleep coming now.

Now, 30 hours. I counted them. No, I tried to count them.

I did the math. Crazy math. I added up 86,400 seconds to a day. That's 1,440 minutes. I tried to add six more hours and do the math with my eyes closed. I failed and tried and failed and tried.

Whipsaw. Concrete to pour.

Whipsaw. Absence and presence.

Whipsaw. At one.

It, the baby, Jennifer. What was her sacrifice?

Until pre-dawn grayed the room.

✳✳✳

Morning numb. Coffee and more coffee. A coffee jag. Almost normal. Almost routine. Morning sun. Kitchen. Mitt gurgling. Annie humming. The surf of static fading from my ears. The absence of sleep was steadily being replaced by the presence of the day.

Jill handed me a folder. "You brought this home yesterday."

It was the folder Joel gave me. It returned me to that moment in my office. The urgency in his voice. "Don't talk to Farley." I one-handed the folder open and read.

It was a copy of Farley Haman's military record. Several pages, and one was marked.

Farley's duty stations, the record of his overseas placements, all of them.

I went through the list. Farley Haman had never been in Vietnam.

E. Farley Haman: War Vet, Mr. Combat, Leader of Men.

E. Farley Haman, who burnished himself like a medal, was a fraud.

✱✱✱

The commute. I left the house. My house. Our house. Instantly, the pursuit came out of hibernation. Footsteps behind me while I was driving a car.

Then, voices. New, impenetrable, murmuring voices. Fast and low. "Listen to me. Listen to me. Listen to me."

They came in waves. "Listen to me. Listen to me. Listen to me."

I lowered my rear-view mirror so that I could see the back seat.

Empty. Stupid to crazy. Footsteps behind me.

The voices followed me from the parking lot and through the front door. I left Helen the Receptionist in my wake. I may have been rude. There was no stopping. No talking. Something new was pushing upward against the trapdoor in my brain. Or had it been there all along? I feared what was on the other side. I was being pursued in my own head, now.

"Listen to me. Listen to me. Listen to me."

Stop it. Stop it. Stop it.

Elevator. Farley. The Gauntlet.

"Listen to me. Listen to me. Listen to me."

Stop it. Stop it. Stop it.

I passed Farley. He followed, saying something. Waving something. I just wanted to close the door, thinking maybe this, the crazy, all of it, would go away. Farley followed me into my office. He closed the door, but it didn't close the trapdoor.

Fear. Panic. Stop. Wait.

No. Focus. Focus. Have to focus.

Breathe. I focused.

Exhale. I glanced.

Farley looked like he was trying to be taller. Chest out, touch of swagger. Whatever it was, I wasn't buying. No thanks, not today.

Whipsaw. Janus. Time, duality, beginnings and endings.

Whipsaw. Buried treasure.

A question awaits you.

Focus. Find something, anything, to focus on.

I turned away and moved to my drawing table. My second home. My back was to the room. Farley talked to my back.

"I got a call from E&P yesterday."

He sounded like he was in a barrel. I managed a reply.

"E&P?"

"Editor and Publisher."

Whipsaw. It to you to thou.

"Editor and Publisher?"

"Andrews, you don't know anything, do you?"

Tough question, considering the trapdoor in my head.

Focus. I didn't need this. I couldn't hide the we're-running-out-of-patience tone in my voice. My back was still to him. If I answered, maybe he would go away.

"Just...just what is it?"

Whipsaw. Absence and presence.

Whipsaw. At one.

Leave me alone.

"It's the journal of record for the newspaper industry."

"No, I mean, what is it? What do you want?"

A question awaits you.

And then it stopped. I don't know why. Had I made it stop? I focused again. The static faded. The pulsing in my ears faded. I turned to Farley. He continued. "They're running a story on you in the next edition. The writer called me for a quote."

At first, he lost me. Then the aha moment. The syndicate deal. This meant I had inked the contract. Signed it without telling Jill while I was in another reality. If she had known, she would have mentioned it. I turned my head and gave him my so-what look.

"I told the writer to give me a day or two. Then I told his editor I might have a feature story on you they might want."

He laid a sheaf of papers on my desk, paper-clipped and typewritten. Very tidy and neat.

I scanned. His byline. It was about me. About my life in Nebraska. There it was, the arrests, the disorderly conduct, all of it. Then there was the source who said I impregnated a local girl and skipped town.

A source. Not enough for a full-blown news article, but enough for Haman and certainly enough to spook the syndicate boys. "Flyover country. Family values."

To top it off, a photo of my profile through the window of a police car. Back seat. Chicago boxcar. Sullen. Guilty.

Enter Joel, with overflowing hair and overflowing clothes and toting an overflowing box. His eyes, overlarge behind the glasses, grew even larger as they went from mine to Haman's and back. He started to back out.

Haman stopped him. "It's good that you're here, Joel. No secrets here between you two, right? Buddies, right? You can be a witness. Yes, a witness."

Joel stayed. His eyes rested on Haman's sheaf of papers atop my drawing table. The folder with Haman's military record was also on the table. Joel's eyes went from mine to the folder and back. I gave him my not-now look.

Whipsaw. Time. Duality. Beginnings and endings.

Whipsaw. At one.

Stop it.

Focus.

Haman came back to me. He was enjoying this way too much. "Congratulations on getting the syndicate deal."

He pointed to the sheaf of papers.

"You can keep those. I made several copies. Say, that syndicate. Kansas City, right? The E&P writer who called me said that the syndicate hopes you will appeal to people with middle-class family values. You know, God and country."

Whipsaw. Concrete to pour.

A question awaits you.

Stop it.

Focus.

I focused. Time to get to the point here. "So, what is it you want from me?"

"A quote."

"A quote from me."

"Yes. Good journalism compels me to offer you a chance to respond to the charges."

"Compels."

I didn't say more, mostly because I couldn't. It dawned on me that I just didn't care. I must have let too much time pass, because Farley pressed me again.

"So, I can write that you refused comment on this?"

No reply.

"Then perhaps I can get your opinion."

"Opinion."

"Your opinion. Before the syndicate starts an expensive campaign to launch your cartoons nationwide, should they know about this."

He pointed to the papers. I said what came into my mind.

"You're wearing elbow patches."

Not sure who was more confused, Haman or Joel or me.

"A corduroy sport coat with elbow patches. Joel, I believe he is a P…H…D."

Haman tried to make himself taller again as I jammed down the trapdoor in my brain.

Exhale.

You could tell he didn't know what to say, so he spoke. "So, you have no opinion?"

"Nope. And I have a witness to the absence of the presence of an opinion."

I knew Haman would leave. I also knew he would come back. He hadn't gotten what he wanted. What that was, I could only guess, but I was pretty sure it had to do with me weeping, groveling, and pleading.

He did leave. Joel waited until the door closed. He walked over and cracked it open. No, Haman wasn't eavesdropping.

He whispered anyway. "Why didn't you show him the folder?"

"Joel. The answer is…the answer is, I don't know."

This was true. But part of me, a big part of me, told me I would know soon enough.

"You could have trumped his hand. It could all be over. What if he sends that article. Where would he send that article?"

"E&P. It's the journal of record for…"

"Matt, I work in the library. I know what E&P is."

I gave Joel my take-it-to-the-bank look.

"He won't send it."

"What's to stop him?"

"He wants to see me suffer first."

No, that wasn't all of it. Maybe somewhere inside his

corduroy jacket was a living, breathing human being. Now that we'd been face to face on the matter, maybe ruining me didn't feel so good to him.

Joel gave me his gotta-go look. "Well, you still have your trump card."

Joel didn't go. One more thing to say. "What do you think it means, I wasn't here? I mean, my pager. It wasn't me?"

"It went to a pest control company."

"Okay, well, at least we know you can call on me here. You know, on this side."

I could tell Joel was trying to simplify things for me. It didn't work.

Joel still didn't go. He had one more one-more-thing. "You don't look good. You don't look…right. You want me to take you home?"

"I'm fine."

You could tell he didn't believe that. I gave him my I-mean-it look.

Exit Joel. I turned back to my drawing table. This wasn't going to be easy. It wouldn't be another evergreen 'toon. Couldn't be. I needed to focus. I would have to keep the trapdoor in my brain closed and barred.

I looked down at my desk. While I'd been sitting there with my back to Haman, and while the voices in my head had been so relentless, I had sketched the Modigliani of Abby.

If you are going to publish an opinion about something, you should know what you are talking about. This is a point that too few newspaper people seem to grasp, but one I made a point of following.

Except, I didn't know what I was talking about. Not lately, anyway. My only contact with the news since, since I don't know when, had been a country music radio station in Kansas, and there it was livestock prices and soybean yields.

I tried to catch up. I would manage to keep my brain door barred. Read the day's headlines, the op-eds, anything.

Impossible. Nothing. Nothing seemed to matter. Words sliding down a drain. No, what mattered to the rest of the world didn't matter to me. Not today. I knew the only thing I would draw that day was the Modigliani of Abby.

A mental loop. A form that refused to take shape. Draw and erase. Draw and erase.

To the evergreen file. One 'toon remaining. A sinking ship. I'd saved the worst for last.

✳✳✳

There are worse things than having nothing to do. I just never could think of any. Now, it was worse than worse. I passed through the door of the newspaper.

Sidewalk. Cold. Lonely islands of ice clinging to the pavement. Transparent. Desperate. Black underneath.

The sidewalk air cracked the trapdoor in my brain. Now it had my full attention. There was nothing else to consider. The pursuit came out of hibernation again.

A question awaits you.

Diversion. The gym. I'd go to the gym. I hadn't been to the gym in a week. I could walk there from here.

Busy. I'd be busy. I'd stay busy. Keep my back to the wall.

I got to the entrance at the gym. No. Now that it was in front of me, the thought of entering cast a spell of fatigue. It seemed futile. I turned away.

Back to the trapdoor.

Okay, the diner. Halfway there. No. No, and no. Chills. The scene of the crime. I would never go back there.

Back to the trapdoor.

Walk somewhere else. Walk. Yes, I would walk.

Every street sign, every shop window, every passing sound spun me in a circle. No sanctuary.

Whipsaw. Sunrise smile.

Sleepless eyes.

Whipsaw. Snow angel.

I walked. Now a second set of footsteps or maybe the echo of my own.

Whipsaw. Buried treasure.

Whipsaw. It to you to thou.

Whipsaw. Sunflowers.

Whipsaw. Put yourself into us.

I walked. Footsteps behind me. Nobody there.

Whipsaw. Pray for rain.

Whipsaw. Absence and presence.

I walked. Footsteps behind me. Nobody there.

A question awaits you.

I walked. Footsteps. Nobody.

Whipsaw. At one.

I walked. Footsteps. Nobody.

Whipsaw. Twenty-three, Sixty-nine, Five.

Whipsaw. Janus.

Whipsaw. It to you to thou.

Whipsaw. At one.

I walked. Footsteps. Nobody.

A question awaits you.

Whipsaw. At one.

I walked.

Whipsaw. At one.

Whipsaw. Abby. Firehose. Jill. All of me. Janus.

Whipsaw. Sunlit faith.

Whipsaw. Longing and shame. Pray for rain.

Whipsaw. Buried treasure.

Whipsaw. It to you to thou.

Whipsaw. Pride, greed, lust envy, gluttony, wrath, sloth, goldfinch.

Whipsaw. At one. Twenty-three, Sixty-nine, Five. At one. Twenty-three, Sixty-nine, Five. At one.

I paused. The incoherent static didn't. I looked around. It was dark. I was somewhere near downtown Atlanta. Ringing in my ears. People looked at me. I could see their apprehension. No, I could feel it. I'd been talking to myself and it appeared that I'd been loud. I caught my reflection in a window. I had my head in my hands, half my face a specter in the pallor of the streetlight. Sunken eyes above black creases.

Lifeless. Ashen. Aged. Worn. Perhaps insane.

A question awaits you.

I pulled my head from my hands and let the question come in. I had to. I knew it would never go away. It came.

It, the baby, Jennifer. What was her sacrifice?

And there it was, rising in front of me and above me like an ogre. The answer. It had been there all the time, underneath the wanting-to-be-here-but-having-to-be-there yearning and disarray. Underneath my fixation on the dismal me on the other side of the coin, the selfish, ardent, charming, force of nature boy-man who could cast morality aside and get away with it and be pardoned again and again as he brandished his contempt for virtue.

And who was also the one who did the honorable thing at

the crossroads that night in Nebraska.

There was no escaping it. That night, when I drove away from Abby, I also drove away from it, the baby, Jennifer, I created the path that led to a collision with myself in the form of a burning truck rammed into a culvert, leading to the church and Gray.

It, the baby, Jennifer. What was her sacrifice?

Her destruction as a human being purchased my renewal as a human being.

There was a day at work I remember, will always remember. I had penciled and inked my 'toon. It was as good a 'toon as I could produce. It had Matt Andrews written all over it. When I reached for the phone to call a copy boy, I spilled a cup of coffee over the drawing. Instantly, it was too late. I didn't bother to rescue the thing. I watched the lines lose their sharpness and the shapes lose their form until the drawing and coffee stain became one and the same.

At that moment, I had become that drawing. Matt Andrews and a stain, one and the same. I took in my reflection again. You can't measure emptiness.

The raw chill of a January night. Streets making wind tunnels. No sanctuary. No direction. Right. No. Left. No. Forward. No. Back. No.

The footsteps behind me had ceased. They were replaced by hot breath on my neck. I knew if I swiveled in any direction, I would see no one. I turned anyway. Nobody.

I would walk no further. I was no longer being pursued. I was overtaken. Hot breath. Wherever I was supposed to be, this was it. The middle of everywhere.

I knew what I was going to do before I knew what I was going to do.

I knew I didn't want to do it.

No, I did want to do it.

No, I had to do it.

The urge unbidden. Paralyzed and moving at the same time.

My hand. Colorless.

My hand in my pocket.

My hand holding a coin.

My hand with a fifty-cent piece. The fifty-cent piece.

My hand flipping the coin.

A low sawdust chuckle. The hot breath ceased.

Black.

XIII
CROSSROADS

Corn. I could smell it. Fields and acres of it, the nutty, roasted scent as the electric thrill passed, black replaced by moonlight on tall corn. August corn with luminescent silks.

Heat. I could feel it. Dead, late summer night heat.

My hand, unbroken. A lit cigarette. Me in a t-shirt and jeans. At my feet, pavement. Yellow stripes.

And a fifty-cent piece.

A gentle grumble behind me, ebbing and returning. One moment tinny, the next throaty.

I glanced over my shoulder. My truck. My Nebraska truck.

I glanced up. The moon.

I felt stupid. Fatigue. The static, gone. The door in my brain. Nothing pushing. Exhale.

"Welcome back, Kiddo."

I followed the whiskey and sandpaper voice. And I knew him.

Him. The man reclining on a duffel bag. Him. The faceless man with the fedora. Him. The man with no color in the moonlight. Him. The man with a black and white hand. Him.

231

The man with his thumb up in a lazy hitchhiker motion.

Time for a stupid question. "Where are we?"

"Where you've been before."

"What year is this?"

"You are outta time, kiddo."

The hitchhiker rose. He ambled toward me, deliberate and languid, until we were face to face. Mine in the moonlight. His in shadow. He reached over toward my shoulder, slow and easy, and unrolled a pack of cigarettes from my sleeve. He pulled one out and put the pack in his shirt pocket. He took my cigarette from my hand and lit his off the burning end. He offered to return it. I gave him my no-thanks look.

Flick.

"Which way ya goin' kiddo?"

"What is this?"

"This is what it is."

"Why? Why are you doing this to me?"

"Because I can. And it's my job. Which way ya goin'?"

I felt the old Nebraska stubborn rising. I stepped toward him, menacing. He laughed that musical, dreadful sawdust laugh. He looked me up and down. At least, I thought he did. The hat moved. His face stayed in shadow. I saw his mouth move.

"What is it you think you're gonna do?"

He was right. Whatever this was, was bigger than me.

My turn. "What do you want from me?"

"I want you to say which way you're goin'."

"I...I don't know what you mean."

"Yes, you do. Ya gotta choose, man. You can't keep this up. Nobody can. It's wearing me out, too. Back and forth and back and forth and back and forth."

"You go to Hell."

"Where I'm goin' ain't the question."

I did know what he meant. I did know what the question was. I did know what he wanted from me. Then it started to rise like the grind and rumble of the truck. The sound. It began to move inside my head. The wash and surf of my own pulse in my ears. The swelling murmur of voices under the trapdoor in my brain. The static. The Fear.

He lit another cigarette off the one he was smoking. "What did you think, we were going to do this forever?"

"I want it to stop."

This wasn't true. I was afraid to stop it. Afraid of what could be next.

"One of 'em has gotta go."

Gotta go. Gotta go. The trapdoor again. I pushed back against it. The voices. The voices would say out loud what that meant. Hands and fingers pushing. Tiny fingers. Gotta go. No. I wouldn't listen. I rose up and tried to look him in the eye. His face stayed in shadow.

I spat words at him. "You can't do this."

"You mean, replace something with nothing? Don't kid me, kiddo.

Whipsaw. Mitt, and Annie. Jennifer. Jennifer. Mitt, and Annie.

"Gotta go, kiddo. Gotta go. Time to choose."

Whipsaw. Absence and presence.

"Kiddo, you had your chance before. At one."

I could feel Jennifer's hand in mine. I could feel myself flowing into her. I could feel Annie and Mitt in my arms, the two flowing into me. And then nothing.

Horror. The word is too easy to say. You think you know it,

until you do. It's the finality. Something is about to happen and you can't stop it. You know you will soon bear the unbearable. It is to stand on dry land and be unable to breathe.

For more days than I could count I'd hammered myself with questions about what was real. There was no question now.

Horror forces you to confront it. There is no escape. No sunlit upland awaits you. No hero to the rescue. It's you alone with the hideous, sickening truth of the moment. Dreams paralyze you. Horror disables you.

Time slows. Vision channels. Sound muffles. Colors grow silent. Air goes absent.

Now, there it was. Horror. No air. Heaving. Reeling.

I would beg.

He knew it before I did. He laughed his words at me. "If you are about to say 'please, please, this is unfair,' I don't care."

The low thump swelled to a clamor. The truck idling inside my head. Grumbling. Grinding. Deafening. I put my hands over my ears. No relief. No sanctuary.

Whipsaw. Mitt, Annie. Jennifer.

Whipsaw. Jennifer. Mitt, Annie.

"You're telling me to kill..."

"I'm telling you to pick one or the other. East or West. Heads or tails. The one you pick will stay. The other one goes away."

"Goes away?"

"Never happened. Now pick it up."

"You can't just, just undo a person."

"Oh, really? Why do you think we're both here at this place, now?"

He may have laughed. I don't know.

Pick it up. The coin. The coin at my feet. This couldn't be happening. Yes, it could. It was. The coin at my feet. Finality.

Horror. I couldn't. I didn't even try.

Make it go away.

Whipsaw. Sunrise smile.

Make it go away?

Whipsaw. Snow angel.

Make it go away?

Bile. Churning in my stomach. Pulse. Baleful drumbeat in my ears and head, grinding in the background. Try to breathe. Inhale, nothing. Try to breathe. Inhale, just enough. No sanctuary.

Whipsaw. Mitt, Annie. Jennifer. Jennifer. Mitt, Annie.

And the trapdoor. Unbarred. Crack. Creeping open. Unyielding. The tiny hands and the voices. This time it would open wide, all the way. Horror. Finality. Now the hands would torment me. I surrendered. The hands set the pace.

They opened slowly. Torture. Blackness. Seething.

I was on my hands and knees. I don't know how I got there. I couldn't feel the road.

Feet, I could see his feet and the stripe in the road and the coin. I could see them through the tears, like rain on a window.

"Pick it up."

"Please. Please, I beg you. Please, no."

They weren't words as much as sobs. Ruin poured through me. I didn't fight it. I couldn't fight it.

The coin. The terrible coin, inches from my hand. It may as well have been a mile. I would never reach it.

"At one, kiddo."

Whatever he wanted, I would give him. What was it? "I don't know what you mean. I don't know what you want."

"At one."

Nothing from me.

"Okay, kiddo. I'll do it for ya."

Through my rain window eyes, I saw the black and white hand reach down. It flicked away the cigarette and picked up the coin. My eyes stayed on the road beneath my hands.

"Here ya go, kiddo."

I heard a ting, and then nothing. Silence. Silence for I don't know how long.

The coin dropped down in front of me. Thunk. Overloud. It bounced. Loud and muffled at the same time, echoing. It bounced again. Slow-motion. It spun in hypnotic, drunken revolutions.

I slapped my right hand over it. I stayed on all fours. I didn't look up.

The whiskey voice. "Well, let's see it."

I didn't move my hand. I could see my sweat and tears dripping onto the road.

The whiskey voice. "Are we just gonna stay here forever? You gotta be uncomfortable down there."

"I can't. I can't. Me. Take me. Take me instead."

I meant it. I meant it more than anything I've ever said or ever will say.

"Doesn't work that way. At one."

I stuck my left hand into my jeans pocket. My Nebraska jeans. And there it was, my Nebraska pocketknife. I dug it out and pulled the blade open with my teeth.

"Then I'll take myself."

I reached to slice my wrist. His foot came down on my hand. The knife skittered away.

"Against the rules, kiddo. You do that and everybody goes away. At one."

Defeat. Sooner or later, I would have to move my hand. It

was inevitable, but still, I resisted. No sanctuary.

The trapdoor in my brain fell wide open. A sound emerged, a low sound in a fog. It swelled and the pitch got higher and louder until it rattled inside me.

I no longer had control over my hand. I watched, paralyzed as it came away from the pavement. There it was, the coin. The rattling in my head became quaking. Piercing. Babbling. Savage. Mad.

It was the sound of my own scream.

His foot lifted off my other hand. My eyes carried skyward. The Black and White Man stood over me. He tipped his fedora back and his face took form in the moonlight. The features gathered through the rain window before my eyes. They formed and returned as teardrops washed over them.

He put a cigarette to his lips. He struck a match.

An eye. A squint. A cheek. Half a face. Red lit.

I'd seen it before.

In a mirror.

It was my own.

He took a long drag off the cigarette and gave me an untranslatable look. He exhaled and spoke as the smoke slowly pulled him inside out.

"Atone."

He passed into the air with it. He was gone. I was gone. Black.

XIV
DAY ONE

I love my work. I love working. I'm really good at it. Today would not be an evergreen day. I would produce a worthy 'toon.

Maybe.

I felt good, considering. I'd had sleep, lovely sleep. I was on my way to restoration. No, something else. Renewal. My office, my table, my lamp, me. Fresh.

Enter Joel, who the day before followed me out of the building because "he didn't trust his pager." Joel, who followed me to the gym and watched me turn away from the door. Joel, who trailed me while I walked Atlanta, stupid gone to crazy. Joel, who came to me when I fell, lifting me up from my hands and knees in the gloom and chill of Piedmont Park. Joel, who cleaned me up and gave me a beer and took me home and gave Jill a story about us having one too many after work.

Joel, who listened to my story, all of it. And now Joel, today, still curious.

"Do you want to talk more about it?"

"Someday. I owe you that. Just, just not today."

239

"One thing then. Tell me if my story worked. You know, with Jill.. About the beers and the long night and everything."

"It did. She actually thinks I should do that kind of thing more often. Drinks with the boys."

"You aren't the type."

Joel. Perceptive Joel. Deeper than you think Joel.

He tried to lighten things up. "What are you gonna draw today? What's the topic?"

I didn't realize I knew it until I said it. "It won't be politics. I'm not sure how it will read, but the image will be a guy coming out of a gazebo."

Only Joel would let it go at that. He came to me and placed a slip of paper on my table. "I was going to give this to you yesterday. Decided not to."

I didn't see what was on it. We were interrupted by E. Farley Haman thrusting through my door. He looked serious. He didn't acknowledge Joel.

"No more prevarication, Andrews."

I didn't want to do the dance with him. He filled me with a weight and a sadness. No, it was pity. He made me tired.

He waved the familiar sheaf of papers, which now included his finished article. "I'm sending this today. It's your last chance to respond."

Silence. You could hear my illegal coffee maker bubbling. Joel and I exchanged a glance. I reached out my hand. Farley handed me the sheaf of papers. I placed them on my table.

I lifted a folder from my table. Joel's folder, containing Farley's military record.

I held it out to Farley. Silence. He eyed the folder. He took it and leafed through the pages. When he found the marked page, he took a deep breath. He seemed smaller.

240

No, he was smaller.

He eyed Joel, then me. "Well, Andrews, I guess this is your leverage."

"No. No, it isn't."

Joel gave me his are-you-nuts look. Farley gave me a blank stare.

I spoke gently and sincerely. On any other day, sincerity with Farley would surprise me. Not today. "Your story is true, Farley. I did all those things and more. And there's more to my story, but you don't deserve to hear it."

Farley was still blank, but I had his attention.

"When you are young, you make decisions. You do things. And you think they disappear behind you. They fade to nothing in your rearview mirror. Then you get older and one day you round a bend and there it is, waiting for you."

I handed him his article.

"You might think that your article, my past, is what was waiting for me. My moment of truth. It isn't. It's the other way around, Farley. I was waiting for it. And I waited too long. Far too long."

I pointed to the folder.

"And I think maybe you've been waiting, too. For perhaps far too long."

He seemed to grow even smaller. His eyes searched the room. They searched the floor. No sanctuary.

I didn't offer any. "I think there is a place inside you that needs attention. A place where something should be, but nothing is there."

His eyes rose to meet mine, and from that moment, E. Farley Haman and I shared something.

I was pretty sure we would never like each other, but I knew we would be connected.

For now, though, he had a confrontation to endure, and it wasn't with me.

"The folder is yours, Farley. There is only that one copy. It's yours to carry. As far as Joel and myself are concerned, this never happened. It doesn't leave this room."

I gave Joel my are-we-okay-with-this look. He was. Exhale.

I needed to release Haman. I had work to do. I had a life to embrace. "Do with it what you will. The same goes for your article about me. Me, I don't care. You, well, good luck."

I was done with him. Time for goodbye. "Now, if you'll excuse me, I've got concrete to pour."

Haman had no idea what I meant, but he understood we were done. Wrong, not done. He might follow that detour sign someday. He might ask for directions.

***

The slip of paper Joel handed me that day contained a phone number. Abby's phone number. Joel had found her. He used the same Nebraska librarian Farley had used to start the trace of my past. The area code was Kansas City.

I had to know, but I held the little paper for weeks. I kept it in my wallet. I pulled it out every day, only to replace it.

What to say? Where to begin? Would she want to hear my voice? Would she want to be reminded of Nebraska? Did she have regrets? What happened? What finally happened?

It would have to come from her. I had to know. The longer I waited, the more I knew the day would come.

When it did, I was at my drawing desk.

She answered on the fourth ring. "Hello?"

"Abby, it's…"

"Matt." She breathed my name. No, she sighed my name. Relief. Sunflowers.

"Yeah, it's…it's me. How, how are…"

"I'm fine."

I could tell by her voice it was true. In the Midwest, the answer is always "fine." It's a good answer, a description of spirit and attitude that overcomes the details. Still, you have to know how to interpret it.

Her turn. "How are you?"

"I'm fine, too."

She beat me to my next question. "We have two boys."

And she beat me to the big question. "Ages eight and ten."

Silence. We shared the elephant in the room in silence.

She broke the silence. "And you?"

"A girl, three, and a boy on his way out of diapers. And one on the way."

More silence. All that time I spent delaying the call and I never thought through what I'd say.

She broke it again. "So many years."

It was an opening, and I went in. I told her my story. The night I left Nebraska. Wrecking in Missouri. Gray Jarvis. My sexton years. The Navy. My cartoons. Jill, Mitt, and Annie. Atlanta. All of it except the Black and White Man and his coin. And then I came to the moment I had thought about. The thing I thought had to be said. Knew had to be said.

"I'm…I'm sorry…"

"Matt."

It was enough to stop me. It was all she had to say. There was absolution in her voice. No, it was her telling me I didn't need absolution, at least not from her. I also knew from that one word that she had been to her own crossroads in the night. One word, worth a thousand pictures.

She broke the moment. "I don't have to ask you how you're doing now. You're famous."

"Famous?"

"Your cartoons. They're in the paper here. You're still doing Modigliani."

Modigliani. She beat me to my next question again. "I still have the one you did of me."

Which returned both of us to that night in Nebraska. Silence again. Not a bad silence. Just silence. The sound of thinking.

She broke it again. "So much to tell."

And she did tell me her story. She was married and happily so for twelve years. Left Nebraska for art school. Found her dance partner, and now she was an art therapist at a school for people with disabilities. She was still painting. I could feel contentment in her voice. She was where she wanted to be.

We talked about things great and small. It was a meandering stream of words, easy and natural. A laugh here, a moment of silence there. It reconnected us. I'm not sure that's the right way to say it. It put us both where we needed to be, almost. There was something that I needed to say.

"I never told you that I love you."

I expected a pause on her end. None came.

"You're telling me right now. We're telling each other right now."

There, we'd both said it, in our way, and saying it made small talk seem too small, although we continued to try until the clock ran down. You can only say so much. The business of the present is what truly engages us. Abby and I had only the past. And so, the long farewell. A cascade of promises. We would get together someday. Our families would meet. In fact, we were heading her way. Jill, the kids and I were planning a cross-country tour. Stops in Missouri to see an old friend and have a look at some farm property, then the Grand Canyon, then Los Angeles. There was a piece of art in a museum there. I wanted to put a champagne flute on it. Agreed. We'd get together.

She started heading for the final goodbye. I stopped her. "One more thing."

"Okay."

"Do you remember my studio house in Nebraska?"

"Of course. You never let me clean it."

"Do you remember the way the floor looked?"

"I repeat. You never let me clean it. It was beyond awful. In fact, I took a picture of it. Several pictures actually."

"Do you still have them? The pictures?"

"Somewhere. Yes."

"It would make a great still life, don't you think? Something big. Big enough you can read the details, even the words and numbers. Long horizontal. I'm thinking twelve feet wide. Museum wall stuff. A real statement. You'll turn the concept of a still-life on its head."

Silence on her end. A good silence. She wanted to paint it, I could feel it, but it was a big assignment.

I went on. "There is one thing I think you should do with it."

"So now you're my art director?"

"Well, okay, just consider it a request. Don't change a thing you see in the pictures. Use all of it, as it is. Okay, one change. You can leave out my last name in the places it appears. It doesn't need to be there anymore."

I could hear the cogs turning in her brain as our farewell

came upon us. I knew she would paint it. We also both knew we'd never see each other again. My cross-country tour would not stop in Kansas City.

It hadn't been an empty promise. It was just a promise that felt too good to say and hear but could never come true. It would be too much. Too much to contain. I wouldn't put Jill through it. I knew without asking that the feeling was the same on Abby's end.

But even that wasn't the real reason. The real reason was too real. There was a place. A place inside both of us. A place where something should be and there is nothing there. A lacuna. We knew if our eyes ever met again, we'd both see into it.

I clung to the word goodbye as I said it.

Our phones disconnected. Exhale. Another exhale. Push the phone away. Stop. Smaller exhale, and a glance upward.

And it was back to the drawing board. My drawing board. A place where something should be and there is nothing there. Until I put it there. Better better better. Inhale.

I started to draw a goldfinch escaping a cage.

THE END

Acknowledgements

I WOULD like to thank Tom Weiss, who played the long game and tucked FLIP into a drawer until the right day came along, and who then became a skilled and perceptive editor. I would also like to thank my Early Reader Squad – Lyn Day, Jim Ellison, Tom Mason, Lynn Clark, Dave Stinson, Jim Dudley, and Brian O'Neill – who were dragooned into reading the story as it developed, and who told me what worked and what didn't. Special thanks to Conservatarian Press, just for being there. Extra special thanks to my dance partner for life, Becca, who read and read and read, and then pestered me until I gave in.

About the Author

STEVE STINSON is an artist and writer in Southwest Virginia, where he lives with his patient wife in the world's smallest five-bedroom house. He has published thousands of drawings and stained his share of canvasses with a misguided brush. He got his first writing gig at age 16, producing headlines for the daily paper in Fulton, Missouri, a place that will always remain his hometown. When he was young and limber, he was a juggler in children's shows. Today, he is known as "Bebop" to his many grandchildren, all of whom are reasons for America to be hopeful. He thinks all things look better from the seat of a bicycle, that white bucks are required at Easter, that birdsong is heaven's whisper, and that Rachmaninoff's Sympony No. 2 is the sound of thinking. Given his druthers, he'd choose to be dancing in the kitchen with his bride.

Also by Steve Stinson:

Adult non-fiction:
Bullet Bill Dudley: The Greatest 60-Minute Man in Football
Children's fiction:
Grumpypants
Where Kent Went
Darien the Crustatarian
Squiffy & the Vine Street Boys in 'Shiver Me Timbers!'
Hay-Hay's Dog Has Her Day-Day
Whit's Matching Shoes
Ice for Rent – Bad Poetry in Motion
Owen's Choice
Go, Trippy, Go!
Visit his website: www.stevestinson.com

Made in the USA
Columbia, SC
04 February 2024

30864484R00143